Pr — D1049099 — **ozen**

"*A Deadly Dozen* is filled with intrigue, wit, and mesmerizing twists!
A lethal treasure trove that offers 12 solid gems, with a shocking new
tale from Agatha Award nominated author Kris Neri, as well as
celebrated author Nathan Walpow's dazzling 'Push Comes to Shove.'
What's more, this Dozen offers many astonishingly diabolical debuts,
from a perfect locked-room jewel by Phil Mann; to Gay Toltl Kinman's
charming pair of librarian-in-training sleuths; to the clutchingly clever
'Driven to Kill' by Jamie Wallace. Read them all and enjoy."
—Jerrilyn Farmer, award-winning author of *Killer Wedding*,
latest in the Madeline Bean Catering Mystery series

"A 'how to' murder manual disguised as a great short story collection.
A terrific anthology—be alarmed, amused, horrified,
and learn how to murder!"
—Claire Carmichael, author of *Under Suspcision*,
latest in the Carol Ashton detective series

"For anyone who's ever lain awake at night fuming over life's injustices,
big and small, twelve talented authors offer wickedly inspired tales
of wrongs righted in very unexpected ways. These are more than
well-crafted stories guaranteed to keep a reader up at night,
cackling with secret delight. No, indeed. Revenge
has never seemed so sweet. Or feasible . . ."
—Taylor Smith, author of *Random Acts* and *The Innocents Club*

"*A Deadly Dozen* is a tangy stew of plotters, connivers, back-stabbers,
and perpetrators. An enjoyable, entertaining mix of short stories sure
to leave you wanting more after devouring this offering."
—Gary Phillips, author of *The Jook*

OTHER BOOKS FROM
SISTERS IN CRIME/LOS ANGELES

Desserticide aka Desserts Worth Dying For (1995, Out of print)
edited by Claire Carmichael McNab, Paulette Mouchet & Mary Terrill

Murder by Thirteen (1997, ISBN 1-890768-15-4)
edited by Priscilla English, Lisa Seidman & Mae Woods

Desserticide II aka Just Desserts and Deathly Advice (2000, ISBN 0-9679037-0-X)
edited by Diane Jay Bouchard & Gay Toltl Kinman

DEADLY DOZEN

TALES OF MURDER FROM MEMBERS OF SISTERS IN CRIME/LOS ANGELES

edited by

SUSAN B. CASMIER
ALJEAN HARMETZ
CYNTHIA LAWRENCE

UGLYTOWN
Los Angeles

First Edition, August 2000

Cover photo by Ron Michaelson

This is a work of fiction. All the characters and events portrayed in this book are fictitous and any resemblance to real people or events is coincidental.

UGLYTOWN AND THE UGLYTOWN COIN LOGO SERVICEMARK REG. U.S. PAT. OFF.

Library of Congress Catalog Card Number: 00-102195

ISBN: 0-9663473-2-3

Find out more of the mystery: www.uglytown.com/deadlydozen

Printed in the United States of America

10 9 8 7 6 5 4 3 2 1

TABLE OF CONTENTS

INTRODUCTION

The murderous Sisters are at it again. Horrendous deeds are splattered across the mystery landscape, from Malibu to Amsterdam, in this new anthology from the members of the Los Angeles Chapter of Sisters in Crime. The dozen deft tales have just a few things in common. All involve murder, the ultimate crime. And they all surprise the reader or end with a twist, in the best tradition of the mystery short story.

Edgar Allan Poe could not have predicted that the genre he created in 1841 would be so *satisfying* that it would flourish to this day. When Poe wrote "Murders in the Rue Morgue," in a few thousand words he invented the locked room puzzle; introduced the first detective, Auguste C. Dupin; and used logic and deduction to solve the shocking crime. "Poe invented the detective story," said Joseph Wood Krutch, "that he might not go mad." Perhaps at 3:00 a.m. our reader, cursed with insomnia, an aching tooth, or a broken love affair, will turn these pages to keep sane.

WOMEN AND MURDER

When did women dip their hands into bloody murder—as criminals, cops, or storytellers? It was earlier than you'd think, in the years between Dupin and Sherlock Holmes.

After London's Metropolitan police force was formed in 1820, a new class of celebrities emerged. Policemen, former and practicing, began writing their memoirs and they became the Victorian equivalent of rock stars.

Fictionalized accounts followed, and in 1864, *The Female Detective* was published. The book, written by Andrew Forrester, Jr., a minor British detective story writer, is hard to find today. Too bad, because this casebook of seven mysteries is solved by the first professional female detective, the fictional Mrs. G. of the Metropolitan police. Mrs. G. uses ratiocination, preceding Sherlock Holmes, who first appeared in "A Study in Scarlet" in 1887. Her short stories are narrated in the first person, a technique that mystery writers use for its immediacy to this day.

The "Had-I-But-Known" school emerged at the start of the 20th Century. Mary Roberts Rinehart and her imitators created romantic heroines involved in mysteries, though not always detecting.

The 1920s and 1930s became the Golden Age of classic mysteries, although most of the marvelous women mystery writers chose men as their detectives, professional or amateur: Dorothy L. Sayers with Lord Peter Wimsey, Margery Allingham with Albert Campion, Mignon G. Eberhart with Lance O'Leary, Ngaio Marsh with Inspector Roderick Alleyn, etc.

If not for the example of Agatha Christie's Miss Marple, potential women sleuths would have limped into their dotages with nothing more appalling than a dropped stitch to occupy their under-utilized minds.

In 1932, Dashiell Hammett gave us Nick and Nora Charles. Later, Frances and Richard Lockridge kept murder breezy with Gerald and Pamela North, as did Craig Rice with Jake Justus and Helene Brand.

These were puzzles topped with froth, with madcap detective teams who thrived on murders and martinis, and who helped America laugh a little through the darkest hours of the Great Depression.

Perhaps the greatest escapist mystery came on the edge of World War II. In 1938, Daphne du Maurier's *Rebecca* combined a heroine-in-danger with a setting that was as much a presence as the characters: the magnificent, brooding mansion, Manderley.

The terrible realities of World War II changed the course of mystery and suspense novels forever. Women writers who chose the mystery form began creating novels of character and psychological motivation. It sometimes seemed as if Thomas Hardy were writing "The Hound of the Baskervilles." The best practitioners produced complex studies of detectives and criminals: America's Patricia Highsmith in 1955 terrifying us with the talented and lethal Mr. Ripley; P.D. James with her poet-detective, Commander Adam Dalgliesh of Scotland Yard. As James has explained, her mysteries deal with "the contrivances by which human beings manage to survive psychologically in this world."

Christie and James were equal opportunity mystery writers. Each created a separate series for a male and female protagonist: Christie with Hercule Poirot and Miss Marple, James who introduced Cordelia Gray in *An Unsuitable Job for a Woman* in 1973.

Despite the popularity of a few British women mystery writers, we American cousins did not do as well. Yes, American women were writing about competent women who solved crimes, in increasing numbers in the seventies and eighties. The problem was—as statistics confirmed—reviewers covered fewer mysteries written by women than by men, even though these sold as well, or often better, than new books by men.

ENTER SISTERS IN CRIME

In 1986, led by Sara Paretsky, a group of women writers formed Sisters in Crime to celebrate the work of women in the mystery field and educate the public and the reviewers about their accomplishments. There is now a supportive national network of chapters; the innovations and promotional efforts of both the national organization and the local chapters have had a profound impact on mystery writing for more than a decade. The network provides information, helps publicize its authors, and presents and encourages new voices.

The Los Angeles Chapter of Sisters in Crime (SinC/L.A.) was organized in 1989 by Phyllis Miller, a nonfiction writer and mystery fan. Founding members included authors Wendy Hornsby, Joyce Madison, Gerry Maddren, Carol Russell Law, and Anita Zelman, plus bookseller Terry Baker of The Mystery Annex at Small World Books.

Today, the chapter continues to cover mystery writers' concerns, from forensics to publishing law, at monthly meetings and its biannual "No Crime Unpublished" workshops. In recent years male mystery writers have been welcomed into Sisters in Crime; if not Brothers in Crime by name, we have all become members of the same congenial family. Two of these brothers are represented here in *A Deadly Dozen*.

The first SinC/L.A. publication, *Desserticide*, appeared in 1995. It paired dessert recipes contributed by chapter members with tasty, not to be taken seriously, advice for would-be murderers. A new and expanded edition debuts this year.

Murder by Thirteen, the first SinC/L.A. short story anthology, was published in 1997. Its continuing success is evidence that thirteen literary murders are not enough.

A DEADLY DOZEN

And now, eager reader, here is the second anthology written by the members of SinC/L.A.: *A Deadly Dozen*, mysteries to brighten those darkest hours before dawn. They include hard-boiled, soft-boiled, cozy, suspenseful, character-driven, and classic puzzles.

Some of the contributors are published writers; others are new talents, and this anthology is their first appearance in book form.

Take note of another trend that may upset your value system. In several of the stories there is no punishment for the crime. Some of our murderers just walk away from their dreadful deeds. Is this justice? Is this morality? Or is this simply another sinister device to make you afraid?

—Cynthia Lawrence
for the editors

Information on joining Sisters in Crime
can be found at the back of this book.

ACKNOWLEDGEMENTS

Our thanks to the Anthology Committee, the Board of Directors of Sisters in Crime/Los Angeles, and president Diane Bouchard.

A special acknowledgement goes to Mae Woods whose business acumen, energy, and commitment were indispensable at every stage of the project.

From the beginning, Kevin Gillogly managed the innumerable details involved in putting together a book. He has the gratitude of the editors, as do Gayle Partlow, Kris Neri, and Linda Bivens of Crime Time Books. Attorney Denise Gibbon is an expert on publishing law; many thanks to her for keeping us legal.

Finally, UglyTown principals Tom Fassbender & Jim Pascoe set high editorial standards for the authors and editors. We respect their professionalism and enjoy their friendship.

a DEADLY DOZEN

SENTENCE IMPOSED

Kris Neri

Call it fate, call it chance—either way, it'll change your life. Sometimes you just find yourself staring into a crowd, your gaze floating aimlessly over a sea of faces you won't remember the instant you look away—until one person's eyes seem to grab hold of yours and you make a connection. You can't explain it, but somehow your life and that stranger's become bound together. When I made that link, it was with a little girl.

I nearly lost my life because of it. I might even have taken one.

Bursting across the finish line, I won the race and set a new course record. I'd been paid a hefty appearance fee to do just that, but until I hit the homestretch, I wasn't sure I could pull it off.

Road races aren't my event; I'm a professional triathlete. But my name, Zoe Morgan, carried some recognition in fitness-crazed North County San Diego, where I live, even if I wasn't the race director's first choice as the star attraction. He'd originally lined up the hottest road racer in the country to compete. But when she broke her leg a week before the starter's pistol was set to go off, the panicky race director waved a relative fortune in my face if I would replace her. During the off-season financial crunch, I couldn't afford to be choosy.

I held court just past the finish line, doing the dog-and-pony show for the spectators and the media, when my life took an unexpected turn.

"Zoe, check out this kid sprinting toward the finish line," one of the reporters said. "Her name's April Russell. She's only twelve, if you can believe it. Gonna be something someday."

She already was. I looked at the clock, then at the computerized result board. The kid's time was outstanding. Only one girl finished ahead of her in her age-group, and she was two years older, a lifetime at that age.

The girl nearly collapsed when she crossed the line, and I wondered whether someone should call a medic. A man pushed his way to her side, a big beefy guy who seemed to be shooting for the unwashed look with his longish hair. The man approached the girl with an arm extended, and I figured she was in safe hands.

Until he smacked April so hard, I expected her head to sail off.

"Jeez, do you believe that?" the reporter muttered, stunned. "I'd heard her old man wouldn't tolerate second place."

And I thought I was tough on myself. April's father grabbed her arm to drag her away. But she held firm for an instant and looked into the crowd. That was when her eyes met mine. It would have been hard to miss hers. That pale little face was all eyes. Deep, dark pits of despair.

It was those eyes that haunted me later, when I remembered that, like everyone else who witnessed her father's cruelty, I took no action.

* * *

My stomach felt queasy during the drive home. I told myself it was the milk. I had goofed this morning, at the ungodly hour I drag myself from my bed on race days, when I absently tossed down a bowl of cereal instead of my usual pre-race peanut butter-and-jelly sandwich. I should have remembered that milk and racing didn't always work in joyous harmony for me.

Of course, I'm temperamentally incapable of accepting defeat in a race. So as I sat at the breakfast table, staring at but not really seeing that wretched milk carton, I reviewed every inch of the course in my mind, with as much attention to detail as I gave the Ironman. And it paid off. Only now that sweet victory tasted a little sour.

My wolf-hybrid, Bob, growled when I unlocked my front door. Several weeks earlier, I'd found him tied to a post outside the drugstore along with a sign that read *Mean wolf-hybrid free to good home*. Truth in advertising. Beneath a magnificent coat of rust and silver and snow lived a surly brute. If we'd bonded at all, I probably blinked and missed it.

The greeting seemed no more than I deserved today. Shame that I didn't help that child suffused me. But I had scars of my own, and fear of my own father could still immobilize me.

I dropped my gear bag to the floor and slumped beside it. The rustic walls of my cozy A-frame house drifted away, and it was as if I were hiding again in my childhood bedroom closet, watching the doorknob turn, knowing I'd pay doubly for eluding him.

Some movement of the dog's jerked me back to the present. I reminded myself that I was an adult—and I kept repeating it like a mantra. I searched Bob's angry wolf eyes for understanding, but they just stared back in accusation.

Zoe, I thought, *what's it gonna be?*

* * *

After a sleepless night, I called Peter Miller, the race director, and asked if he'd heard about the incident.

"Heard? Are you kidding, I *saw* it. Dag Russell hasn't changed a bit."

"You know him?"

"Well, it wasn't like we had a relationship; I was just the nerd he tormented in high school."

"Peter, if you know what it's like, why didn't you do something when you saw Russell hit his daughter?"

"Didn't you hear me, Zoe? If the guy creamed me in high school, he'd probably kill me now. Don't you get it?"

I got it. I just didn't want it.

I asked Peter where to find the Russell family.

"They left the area when April was a toddler and came back a couple of years ago. I heard they moved in with Joan Russell's mother." He checked the race records and rattled off an address several miles northeast of mine. "I haven't heard anything about Dag working, so he's probably rolling drunks these days."

Nervous laughter bubbled up through my throat.

"I mean it, Zoe, don't tangle with him. If you feel you gotta do something, just call Child Services. Let them handle it."

I told Peter he was probably right. I looked up the number for the agency, but I hesitated calling it.

I put Bob on his leash for his daily run, but instead of running our normal route, we took a slow jog toward the address Peter gave me to scope it out. I guessed which house it was even before confirming the address. Weeds as high as the windowsills and more oil on the driveway than the Valdez left in the Gulf of Alaska.

Not wanting to gape, I continued around the block. To my

surprise, since it was during the school day, I spotted April there, running intervals along a stretch of grass in a seedy park. Close up, she looked an awfully young twelve, and there wasn't enough fat on her slight frame to slick a frying pan. No wonder she was thin if she always followed strenuous races with such tough work-outs.

Our eyes met again, and I thought I saw recognition in hers. Yet when I greeted her, she lowered her head in awkward shyness and focused on Bob.

"Does he bite?" April asked.

"He might."

When she locked her haunting eyes on his, I tightened my hold on his leash. These weeks had given me a crash course in the challenges of co-habituating with a wolf-hybrid. I'd seen him threaten to reduce people to hamburger for less than staring. This time, he just offered something that, if I didn't know him better, I would have taken for a doggie smile. He didn't even object when April tentatively patted his head.

"Wouldn't it be wrong if he bit someone?" she asked.

How could I explain Bob's sense of right to a kid who knew too many wrongs?

"Justice is . . . more streamlined for Bob than us. No grays, just blacks and whites. He's judge and jury and doesn't tolerate appeals. Sentence imposed immediately."

She frowned at me, confused. I wasn't sure whether she wasn't very bright or if that was just over the head of a twelve-year-old. What did I know about kids?

She flashed a glance at the cheap, oversized stopwatch that dominated her frail wrist and spun away in the direction of the house.

"Wait!" I shouted, desperate for some way to keep her there.

"Aren't you going to stretch? You don't want to tear a muscle, do you?"

She turned back, unsure, but intrigued. I coaxed her into doing a routine there on the grass. She'd apparently never stretched before, though she caught on fast. She wasn't dumb; she just didn't seem to know things. But in a few minutes, time pressed back in on her. She announced that she had to go, and she ran off before I could stop her.

Nice work, Zoe. I looked at Bob.

"Why me?" I blurted aloud. "I've always been a misfit. How can I hope to fix someone else's life?"

I absently tore blades of grass and tossed them viciously into the air. My fingers fell on a child's barrette lost in the grass. It wasn't hers. There wasn't enough hair in the little cap that curved around April's head to need it.

Of course, I didn't have to know that.

I rapped at the door several times. Though I'd seen a yellowed curtain twitch behind the dirty front pane, no one came to the door. I tried the knob. Unlocked. *In for a penny . . .* I let myself in.

My guess would be they didn't entertain often. The worn vinyl floor was so covered with empty beer bottles, fast-food containers, and yellowed racing forms, there was barely a place to stand. The house smelled of mold and rotting garbage. And fear.

April stood frozen at the window, her face a paler shade than the curtain. Some old woman in a rocking chair rocked with all the fury of a panther pacing a cage. The old lady suddenly stopped and looked at me.

"They take my checks, you know, take my checks," she said.

She might be crazy, but I believed her. Russell doubtless took her Social Security. How much can you make rolling drunks?

A younger woman stood at the other end of the room, wearing a faded dress the color of pea soup, which she'd pinned closed where the neckline buttons had been torn off. She was a big, raw-boned woman, who somehow managed to give the impression of being far slighter. Maybe it was having shoulders so round she should have pitched forward. Then again, the fat lip might have contributed to that impression. Alcohol rolled off her in waves.

I extended the barrette and sputtered my excuse for being there, which now sounded even lamer than when I'd thought of it. No one said anything. I looked from April to the younger woman. Joan Russell?

Finally, April said, "Not mine." Judging by the look she gave me, it was her turn to question my smarts.

Despite the debris, there were no books or magazines in the room, not even a TV. No wonder the kid seemed to lack the normal level of awareness; she received no stimulation.

"April, don't you go to school?" I asked.

"That's not April," the old lady said, before she resumed her frantic rocking.

Mrs. Russell just rolled her eyes. "April is home-schooled."

By whom? The bully, the drunk, or the nut?

I drove back the next morning, parked up the block, and waited. I made the mistake of bringing Bob along. Even from that distance, he howled when he saw April as she went out to train, but I stopped him before he attracted attention. Those grueling workouts had to be exhausting the kid. Only the whip kept her turning in good race times.

Dag Russell ambled to his car and tried to start it around mid-morning. It sputtered a couple of times and caught on the third try. He burned rubber when he took off, sailing through a few stop signs without slowing down.

I followed him to some bar along the waterfront in San Diego where all the waitresses wore tight, skimpy outfits designed to squeeze their breasts out the top like toothpaste from a tube. I snagged a table in a dark corner and nursed a beer. Being that close to him gave my stomach an acid wash. Each time his shoulders flexed, I feared he would turn and see me and somehow know what I was up to. I needn't have worried. He just kept belting back drinks, while placing sucker bets on an ESPN soccer game and trying to grope the waitresses.

One waitress sent Russell an ugly look behind his back. When she went out front for her break, I followed her.

How do people learn to bribe effectively? The detectives in books always seem so smooth when they slip the flophouse desk clerk a bill, you'd think they greased it first. Totally clueless, I held a twenty extended from between two fingers as I approached.

She smiled and reached into the pocket of her French maid apron. "Need change, hon? I think I've got it."

I almost wanted to take the change. I felt like an idiot when I told her that what I wanted was information. Apparently, all I needed to do was ask, though she didn't know much, beyond confirming that Russell spent part of most days there, setting records on offensiveness.

"Any idea why he's so obsessed with his daughter winning races?"

She shrugged.

"I can answer that," a male voice behind me said.

My scalp contracted. God, no! Had Russell caught me? Fortunately, it was only the bartender taking his break. He eyed the twenty still clutched between my fingers.

"I was working the day a patron asked us to turn to the broadcast of a marathon. The guy's son won it, and everyone fell all over themselves buying him drinks. I swear, you could almost see the light bulb go on over Russell's head. Next thing I knew, I heard his kid was racing. I never even knew he had a kid. It's not like he talks about anyone but himself."

That explained why he drove her so mercilessly. He wasn't the first parent who craved the reflected glow of his child's athletic victories, though I'd never seen anyone pursue it with such a maniacal vengeance. I figured I'd learned all I was going to, and I had left Bob in the car. The twenty was still out there, with one of them on either side. I sure wasn't about to double it. I looked awkwardly from it to each of them.

"You gonna get rid of him for us, hon?" the waitress asked.

"Gonna try."

"Then keep it."

After dropping Bob off at home, I headed back toward Russell's house. Before reaching it, I spotted Joan about to board a bus a few blocks away. I made a quick U-turn and tucked in behind the bus. It wasn't easy, following a bus. I half-expected the driver to radio the cops. He had to see me pulling over each time he reached a stop. But I would risk jail before I'd miss seeing where she got off.

The bus dropped her off near the Linda Vista section of San Diego, a middle-class neighborhood well beyond the scope of a family that didn't seem acquainted with soap. Maybe she worked as a cleaning lady—wouldn't that be funny? But she turned away from the neighborhood and walked quite a distance until she picked up a trail in the Tecolate Canyon Natural Park, a sprawling natural preserve nearby. I ditched my Jeep and followed on foot.

Joan's going there seemed an impulsive act. She wasn't dressed for hiking in her pinned-together dress and flip-flop sandals, but she kept a good pace and seemed to know where she was headed. There was no hesitation when one trail handed her off to another. A plastic bag swung from her hand, which appeared to be filled with dandelions in bloom. Planting weeds in the woods?

With the brush so dry it cracked underfoot, I dropped back so she wouldn't hear my approach. I'd been keeping her well in sight, even at a distance, till we came upon a thick fan of bushes that grew perpendicularly from the edge of a jagged cliff overlooking a deep rocky canyon. I lost sight of her once she slipped through those bushes.

I hovered at the fringe of the bushes, unsure of whether to keep going or not. Would I lose her if I hung back? She might see me if I slipped through as she had.

I listened, but didn't hear any movement behind. I realized I expected to hear voices. Why would she make that trek if not to meet someone in a secluded spot? I didn't hear voices, but I did hear something.

Someone beyond the shrubbery was sobbing.

So Joan found a place to have a good cry. With her life, I'd cry, too. But why travel so far for it? Russell might object if he saw her, but he didn't seem to hang around much.

For all my tinkering, I hadn't accomplished anything. I didn't know what more I could do, until April herself gave me a hand. I'd described where I lived when we stretched together and invited her to work out with me. I never expected her to take up the offer, but there she was when I returned to the house, stretching on my lawn the way I taught her.

Her face lit up when she saw I'd returned, but she doused it with a splash of despair. Tears burned my eyes.

I know, kid. Never allowing yourself to hope hurts less than disappointment.

Those rare times my father acted like a normal, loving dad still gleamed like diamonds in my mind; that they never lasted cut like diamonds, too. I longed to hide April but knew it wouldn't work. That she was free to run anywhere proved how thoroughly Dag Russell owned her. For April, there were bars on the world.

On impulse, I invited her to come on a trail run with me. There had to be a reason why Joan went to that place to cry. Maybe with April along, I'd find it.

We drove back to Tecolate Park. April was almost chatty when we started out. Well, chatty for her—she spoke occasionally. When the trails narrowed and we could no longer run side-by-side, I encouraged her to go ahead, and just shouted instructions, as I tried to retrace Joan's steps.

April gradually slowed her pace. She was just a little girl—was I wearing her out? She'd doubtless run all the way to my house. But I came to realize from the way she fixed on her surroundings that it wasn't fatigue that slowed her, but a growing awareness of where we were going.

I wasn't prepared for the scream she let out.

"Nooo!" she wailed and crouched on the ground. "Don't make me go there. I'll be good."

She threw her arms around my legs, sobbing into my shins as she whimpered promises to obey. I tried to comfort her, but she sprinted away. She took me by such surprise I lost her in the trails. Would she find her way out? After an exhaustive search of the park, I drove through the surrounding streets, but she was gone.

*   *   *

What a mess I'd made of my determination to help. Why didn't I just call the authorities? I went home feeling completely defeated. That funk might have smothered me if Bob's expectant vigil at the pantry door hadn't reminded me it was past his feeding time.

I filled his bowl and placed it on the floor. I'd learned to jerk my hand away quickly, or he considered it part of his meal. Distracted tonight, I didn't move fast enough. But instead of gobbling my fingers like kibble, Bob hesitated before diving into his bowl and gave my hand a gentle lick.

So needy was I for encouragement, I nearly whimpered. I reduced the feeling to a lump I wedged in my throat as I addressed my own dinner. I'd skipped lunch, and while I wasn't hungry, as a competitive athlete, I couldn't afford to indulge a bad mood like that. Still, neither could I manage anything harder than cereal.

Cereal again? You'd think I'd learn.

I grabbed a box and bowl, banged them down on the table, and went to the refrigerator for milk. I stared at the carton in my hand, remembering how I'd focused on that during my mental preparation before the race. For the first time, I really *saw* that carton.

I gasped and dropped it. Milk flooded the floor, but all I could do was kneel in the pool and read the side of the carton, looking at April's picture. Two photographs, actually—one as a toddler, the other a computer-aged picture depicting how she'd look now. Only the caption identified her as Sandy Collier.

According to the background description, a strange man had stolen Sandy from the yard of her parents' Oregon home when she was three, and she hadn't been seen since. Subtracting the date, I saw she was ten-years-old, not twelve.

No wonder my eyes connected with hers. I'd recognized her,

unconsciously, from staring at the carton that morning.

"That's not April," Joan's mother had said.

Peter Miller told me they left the area when April was a toddler and, after floating around for years, had only just returned.

She wasn't their daughter! They stole a child and stayed on the move. They only came home when they thought enough time had passed for the people in Oregon to have stopped looking and for the people here not to notice the change in the girl.

So where was April?

I raced through the Tecolate trails. Even the shovel that banged against my leg didn't slow me. I had to find what brought Joan Russell to this spot. Please, God, let me be wrong.

For the first time, I slipped past that shade of bushes. The truth was clear when I spotted the little bouquet of dandelions on a mound of dirt that time had almost flattened.

I leaned heavily on the shovel. I could let someone else take it from here. My friend, Lou Peña, a homicide detective with the San Diego PD, would set things in motion. But I'd taken it this far. How could I hand it over without being sure?

Twilight falls fast in winter, and I was losing the light. But I couldn't leave until I knew. I had to dig down more than three feet, but I found a section of fabric first, the pastel print from a baby's dress, its colors muted after all this time. And then, bone.

I staggered away, trying not to vomit in this place that was both sacred and obscene.

I sat there until the sky grew dark and the ground cold.

I returned to April Russell's grave, and waited. I'd gone back to Russell's watering hole this morning and I'd given that waitress a note to pass to him. He would come—I didn't know when—but he wouldn't be able to resist. He knew what he did there.

It didn't take long. I heard him lumbering through the dried grass, wheezing and swearing. That instant, I returned the bunch of dandelions, which I'd moved when I started digging, back to the center of the grave. But I didn't fill in the hole. I wanted him to know I wasn't bluffing.

The clearing beyond the trees was larger than I originally anticipated, with at least fifteen yards from the grave to the edge of the cliff. I went back into the bushes, where I'd tied Bob earlier. I let him off his leash and paused to scratch his mane, looking into those lonely wolf eyes that always kept me at a distance.

"You make your own rules, boy, but please listen to me this time. Do it for her."

I didn't know whether he understood any of the commands I tried teaching him. But there seemed to be an intuitive level of understanding in this animal that shared my life. I had to hope.

The heavy footsteps grew closer. I rushed to the edge of the canyon, clutching my prop, my weapon.

Dag Russell came through tentatively, his eyes hooded, unsure of what he'd find. He looked at me with disbelief. His head turned quickly to the right and left. The bully's sneer only returned when he seemed confident I was alone.

"What happened, Dag? Did April cry too much, wet the bed? Did you just beat her too hard, or did you mean to kill her?" I asked.

"How . . . how did you know?" he stammered.

I held out a duplicate of the milk carton that told the story. "Did you think Sandy's parents would just forget? That they'd ever let it go?" Maybe he really couldn't comprehend what they felt.

I tipped the carton over, spilling the half-gallon of milk on the ground by my feet, just inches from the edge.

His expression became jovial, as he switched on what I'd bet passed for charm in him. "Come on, little lady, we can work this out. I always say there's nothing that can't be fixed."

"That just proves you're stupid, Dag."

He pulled a small, silver automatic from the pocket of his baggy jeans. "Yeah? Who's stupid now? Not so smart now, are ya, little girl?"

Did he have to keep stressing how much smaller I was? My muscles were honed for unusual endurance, but I wasn't a big woman. My heart began to thud erratically within my chest. I felt myself slipping back in time again, to when I trembled before a man-sized shadow that loomed menacingly against my bedroom wall.

Hold on, Zoe. You're all that kid has.

I steadied my breathing, the way I always did when I began to lose the rhythm to fatigue during races.

"You should know I'm not alone, Dag. Did you think I'd come unarmed?" Sounded strong, didn't feel it. I threw an arm out in vague gesture, hoping Bob saw it.

Russell looked over his shoulder. When no one appeared at eye level, his confidence seemed to mushroom.

"Nice try," he said with a jeer.

Bob growled from deep in his belly.

Russell whirled around. Bob's as big as any full-blooded wolf and many times meaner. Someone must have shown that pup the dark side of humanity. I hoped he recognized that quality again now.

The wolf stalked his prey. Slowly at first, then faster, faster. Russell managed to get off one shot at Bob, but in his panic, it went wide. Before he could better his aim, Bob had broken into a swift run. Russell seemed to grasp flight was his only option. He stumbled blindly. He ran straight at me, not seeing anything at first. Then I watched his eyes narrow on the person he blamed for his predicament. As Bob pursued him, Russell directed his massive body at mine.

I could have run from his path; I was quicker than he was. But I'd been running from someone like him for too long. This time, I had to fight.

I knew what he saw when he looked at me: a woman so slight he could wrap one of his meaty paws around her lean arms. He did not see an athlete. Nor a person hardened by the effort of surviving someone so like him.

In his determination not to miss me, he stretched his arm to the side and spread his fingers. I took hold of a nearby branch, but only for balance. He hurled his body at mine, but his feet slipped in the milk-muddy ground. He went down. Still bent on revenge, he grasped my ankle. Panic flickered within me, but only for an instant. With one smooth motion, I flexed my knee, stiffened my leg, and flicked it back over the canyon wall with such speed that Russell couldn't hang on. The momentum that tore his hand loose sent him sliding along that slippery ground and propelled him over the side.

The echo of his screaming lingered in the air longer than the thud his body made when it hit the bottom.

Zoe Morgan wasn't a victim anymore.

I finally placed those calls I kept putting off. Lou, my detective friend, sounded livid. He always did when I pursued things on my own, but never like this.

"Now you've gone too far, *chica*. How could you uncover a

grave and not tell me?" he demanded.

"I figured you'd need a court order or something to pursue it. I didn't." The truth, just not the whole truth.

The D.A. rattled an obstruction-of-justice saber at me. But his threats sounded empty. I sensed they didn't really mind receiving this case packaged as it was. They were still considering charges against Joan. But everyone knew the monster in the horror story lay dead on the rocks below.

Child Services stepped in and acted quickly. I never had a chance to say goodbye. I knew I'd always look for the name Sandy Collier in juvenile race results, but I didn't expect to see it. Running had given me a way of leaving the demons in my dust when I was her age; most days, I still outran them. But while running set me free, it had framed her dungeon. We were still connected in other, more important ways.

Weeks later, I sighed into the darkness and gave up on getting any sleep, as I seemed to do so many nights lately.

I went to the living room and lit a fire to chase the chill from the air. Staring into the flames, I knew I would still be watching them when the dying embers handed off the baton of light to the day beyond the now-darkened windows. After a while, Bob traced my path, his claws tapping against the hardwood floors, until he curled up next to me on the couch. Since that day at April's grave, we'd grown more comfortable with the patterns we shared.

How fitting that we spent these times together. I finally admitted to myself the cause of my insomnia; I was more like Bob than I knew. I never saw grays, either, just blacks and whites. I also declared myself judge and jury and refused to consider appeals. Because of me, the sentence I believed Dag Russell deserved was swiftly imposed.

Wasn't that the real reason I never shared what I knew with the authorities? Hadn't I feared their justice would not be as exacting as mine?

But if it meant anything, I imposed a sentence on myself that day as well. However much alike we were, Bob and I differed in one respect. For while he snored peacefully before the fire, untouched by his choices—I stared into the flames of my own private hell. Yet I also knew that, despite how it made me feel now, I would do it all over again. In the heartbeat of a child.

Kris Neri has published more than forty short stories, two of which have won the Derringer Award for Best Short Story: her humorous mystery story, "L.A. Justice" (which appeared in the previous Sisters in Crime/Los Angeles anthology Murder by Thirteen*), and the dark and edgy "Capital Justice" (Blue Murder Magazine #1). The off-beat amateur sleuth introduced in "L.A. Justice," mystery writer and detective wannabe, Tracy Eaton, returned for a full-length adventure in Neri's first novel,* Revenge of the Gypsy Queen *(published by Rainbow Books, Inc.), which was nominated for an Agatha Award for Best First Mystery Novel. Readers can reach her through her website: www.krisneri.com.*

WIFELY DUTIES

Cory Newman

True to her wifely duties, Lucy would have tonight's meal ready at precisely five forty-five. An ample buffet—sardines, soup, salad, pot roast, mashed potatoes and gravy—stuff that Walt, true to his typical table manners, could glop and slurp, grunt and burp. The man virtually talked to his food: one-way conversations. She'd put up with it for thirty-seven years. And tonight she wanted to give him the kind of food he'd be sure to spit through his teeth and slosh over his lips. Lucy wanted Walter's loudest performance because tonight the pot roast was going to talk back.

Lucy Hummelthorpe had been a good wife. She'd kept the house tidy, put the meal on the table promptly, listened with feigned interest to her husband's rants about the wood chip industry. He was a sixty-three-year-old production manager for a company that made those chips people use as a lawn substitute. Silly dead brown blocks—who grows blocks, anyway? She wanted a lawn and a garden, but Walt got a deal on the wood chips because he worked for Canyon Landscaping Materials Limited and, besides, mowing a lawn might force him to haul his sagging rump from the Lazy Boy after nine straight hours of sports shows on his one day off. Not that much could grow out here but cactus, anyway.

Ten long years ago Walt's old plant closed down, forcing their relocation. They could've stayed in a place where seasons changed and foliage abounded had Walt known anything other than wood chips. That Walter's doctors (a forever growing team he pestered with every little ailment) said it was a good move for his heart problems only clinched the deal.

Lucy herself couldn't even recall the last time she'd seen a doctor. Oh, now and then she'd feel a little pinch in the chest, a tingle in her fingertips, minor things too fleeting to remember. And if she did remember, she knew the pain would be gone once she got to the doctor's office, just like the constant pinging noise in the car engine that goes silent just as soon as you get to the mechanic's. Overall, she was strong, hearty. The selfless and devoted Molinski women had a history of endurance, with the exception of Aunt Beatrice, bless her soul, who just up and keeled over on the rush hour platform of the IRT at the premature age of forty-three.

For the most part, Lucy went about this particular day as if it were any other. Late afternoon she plunked a cassette from her prized Julio Iglesias collection into the stereo. She could never remember the names of his songs, but his silky voice captivated her. She fantasized about him sidling against her with his sleek, masculine frame, crooning into her ears Spanish words she could not understand.

As the music wafted through the modest one-story tract house, Lucy finished dusting the Franklin porcelain figurines, glass clowns and rarely used crystal wedding vases, mopped the diamond-patterned linoleum, vacuumed the olive carpeting, then ground four little blue pills she'd secretly collected from various neighbors' medicine cabinets into a small pan of dark brown gravy, mixing thoroughly.

Walter Hummelthorpe didn't arrive home until six-thirty. Not unusual. Lucy unblinkingly made allowances for his tardiness, never questioning his whereabouts. Nor did she ever suspect a possible affair. Lucy knew Walt had the libido of one of his wood chips, if not their rigidity. No, Walter never pressured her into those wifely duties.

"I'm home." Walter Hummelthorpe grunted the two words in even measure.

He proceeded to the kitchen, awaiting neither Lucy's response nor presence. He sniffed the air indifferently, "Pot roast?"

Poor Walter, Lucy thought, entering the kitchen in a gauzy, low-cut red dress. Couldn't even show passion for his favorite food anymore. As far as she was concerned, she was doing him a favor.

He squinted at her. "That a new dress?"

She nodded. "You like it?"

"Hmmm . . ." his eyes zoned to her cleavage, "sexy." Looking up, he added, "Got it on sale, I hope."

Lucy fumed. If the dress had cost $5,000 it would have been a steal, considering how few nice clothes she'd bothered to buy in the last ten or so years. What was the point? They rarely went out. For her daily activities, her usual light, practical ensembles suited her just fine: comfortable, dispensable. And, just like now, he'd barely notice, barely get a rise.

Not that she cared too much; she'd long since lost her desire for Walter, too. Once, long ago and forgotten, she'd found him rugged and protective, intoxicated by the manly scent of Brut on his neck. Now he held for her as much magnetism as the kitchen chair he was sitting on. During their rare, six-minute bouts of lovemaking, she kept her eyes closed and pretended he was Julio Iglesias.

Lucy grimaced as Walter slithered a sardine through his teeth.

"That Ben Foley," Walter slurped, splashing food off the edges of his spoon, "he screws up again today. Breaks down the damn machine, second time this week."

As Lucy cleared plates, Walter smacked his lips, sucked his teeth, and belched. She clenched her teeth and heaved a heaping plate of pot roast and mashed potatoes down in front of him. True to his ways, Walter plunged into it before she resumed her seat.

"Just two days ago, two days, I told him, 'Don't overload the machine; feed it slowly.' And today he goes and does the same thing all over again. Can you believe such an idiot?"

Of course the question, like most of Walter's, was rhetorical, which was a good thing since Lucy was too absorbed with Walter's mushing and sucking and the task at hand to answer. "More gravy?" she asked, smothering his plate. It was her turn for rhetorical questions.

"Then he has the nerve to ask me . . ." Lucy studied his greasy smacking lips, parting with every other word to reveal pulverizing swirls of pot roast, mashed potatoes, salad, and gravy.

Trancelike, she heaped a second helping of mashed potatoes on Walter's plate, emptying the gravy boat.

Walt glanced at Lucy's plate of pot roast *au jus* and salad. "Aren't you eating any potatoes?"

She told him about a new starch-free diet she was trying from the *Midnight Globe*, how it was the latest rage with the Hollywood stars. She read the *Globe* a lot. And the *National Enquirer*. Lucy wondered how it was all those other readers kept losing twenty-two pounds in ten days or encountering space aliens. She read *Cosmopolitan* a lot, too, and wondered why she, unlike most of its readers, never discovered g-spots and multiple orgasms.

"Yeah, maybe I ought to cut down on 'em, too." Walter patted his pot belly and burped. Then he took another forkful.

Lucy smiled a Mona Lisa grin. That's it, clean your plate real good, Walter, she thought, her heartbeat quickening.

Suddenly a vague look of confusion came over Walter Hummelthorpe's face as his gaze fell to her cleavage and clung there. His breathing grew heavy, his eyes fixed on her ample bosom. He laid his fork down on his emptied plate.

It was working, Lucy smiled, sauntering suggestively out of the kitchen toward the bedroom. She stopped at the stereo, snapped in good old Julio.

Walter followed her like Pavlov's dog, panting at her gently sashaying hips.

"Let me just turn up the volume here," Lucy drawled seductively.

Walt was no big fan of music, particularly of Julio Iglesias, but given his burgeoning excitement he was loathe to say 'no' to anything.

There was a gleam in Walter's eyes that Lucy hadn't seen in years as he led her urgently to the bedroom, to what, if all went as planned, she knew would be his last performance.

When the police found Walter Hummelthorpe's dead, naked body the next day, their assumptions were pretty much what his wife had counted on. "These old folks," Officer Logan sighed to his partner, "Can't be doing what a young body can." The apparent cause of death—massive heart failure—would be confirmed by an autopsy and validated by several doctors attesting to Walter Hummelthorpe's history of angina and related heart ailments. Were a toxicology report deemed necessary—which was hardly the case in a community where senior citizens' deaths were a weekly fact of life—it would reveal significant trace elements of the virility drug Viagra—something also not uncommon in the community, easily verified by a look in four out of five neighbors' medicine cabinets.

"Well," Officer Cole sighed back, almost enviously, "I guess if you gotta go, this would be about the best way."

The officers looked at the body lying underneath Walter's. The coroner's ruling on this one would also be massive heart failure, again unexceptional considering the deterioration and blockage of so many aortic valves and arteries, though in this case no recent medical history existed for backup.

"She sure looks like she had a happy ending, too," said Logan.

Indeed, Lucy Hummelthorpe died with a smile on her face and a Julio Iglesias song in her heart.

Cory Newman *is currently working on a mystery novel series and a comedic screenplay. She also freelances in editing and development. "Wifely Duties" is Ms. Newman's first publication. She credits her family for fostering both her pursuits and good table manners.*

PUSH COMES TO SHOVE

Nathan Walpow

Thumper's finishing move was called The Thump. It started out like a power slam, but then he would twirl his opponent around so the guy would go face-first into the mat. After each match, Thumper's victim would just lie there, and they'd get a stretcher and carry him off. Thumper would act real sorry and walk halfway back to the dressing room beside the stretcher, then suddenly run back to the ring, put his rabbit ears back on, and get a big pop from the crowd.

I got mixed up with Thumper at a TV taping. Each of the jobbers, me included, had at least three matches, so Lou Boone, the promoter, could build up enough tape to keep the fans going for a few weeks. I'd already had my matches, two squashes and one where they let me put on a few martial arts moves before getting my ass kicked.

Thumper's match was after my last one. His opponent was some new guy whose name I never caught. A jobber. They were still building Thumper up to face some real competition.

After the Thumping I watched on the monitor in the dressing

room as they carried the guy off. Then I went to take a leak before driving back to the motel. But I walked the wrong way and ended up near an exit. I saw them carry the jobber out through a door into the parking lot and dump him into a car. They were handling him like a sack of potatoes.

I forgot about going to the john and ran back to the dressing room to see what the hell happened. But when I got there, Tommy Bufone said Lou wanted me to take the Thumped guy's place in a tag team with Tommy against the Barrister Brothers. The extra money sounded good. I could find out about the guy later.

The Barristers were major heels, so I got to be a good guy for the only time that night. I put on my good-guy tights. No one in the crowd ever noticed I wore a different outfit depending on who I was against, but I didn't care. It helped me play the part better.

Of course, the payoff was the same. I got beat up and pinned. Tommy got to drag me out of the ring.

After the card was over I started asking around about the wrestler who'd been Thumped. I spotted Joe the Greek Pappas, the heel on the announcing team. "What happened to the new guy?"

Joe caught me with the glare they called the Evil Eye when he was still in the ring. "He's fine," he said.

"Where is he?"

Another Evil Eye. "He should be back next week in Springfield." He pushed open the gray metal exit door and walked out into the rain.

I stared after him for a second, then walked back to get my stuff, and there was Lou holding my duffel bag. He's shorter than he looks on TV, and skinnier, and paler. He tossed the bag to me.

"Good work tonight," he said. "I really liked how you sold that double clothesline from the Barristers. The crowd ate it up."

"Thanks."

Lou held his glasses up to the light like he was checking if they were clean. "What do you think of Thumper?" he asked.

"He's pretty big." I could never think of what to say around Lou.

"The fans like him a lot." Now he was wiping his glasses on his tie. "He's the best thing we've had in a long time. I wouldn't want anything to mess that up."

He put on his glasses and pulled on his raincoat and said, "I was thinking maybe it's time to give you a push."

Talk about something coming out of the blue. I was a jobber. I made my living losing. And I knew I didn't have whatever it was that made some wrestlers go over with the crowd. But that magic word "push" made me forget all that.

"You think so?" I said.

"I just need time to think up a gimmick for you. Probably not by Springfield, but by the taping after that I should have something. Then maybe I'll put you in with Illegal Alien." Illegal was a jobber-to-the-stars. He always beat the regular jobbers, but when somebody got a push Illegal was usually the first one who lost to them.

"There's only one thing," Lou said.

"Name it."

"I want you to forget the new guy." Lou gave me a stare that made Joe's Evil Eye look wimpy.

I thought about it a second. Then I did what any jobber would have done.

"Sure, Lou," I said. "Consider him forgot."

* * *

People think it's easy being a jobber. They figure all you have to do is act like you're getting beat up for a while, then you make like you're helpless while the superstar pins you, then you limp out of the ring and collect your pay and go home.

What they don't think about is how you feel outside the arena. You know it's all phony, and your friends and family know, but people on the street don't sometimes. Some of the fans, the ones we call "marks," think this stuff is real. They stop you on the street and say, "You should give it up" or "You'll never win," and they laugh a stupid little laugh and walk off. And you want to call them back and tell them it's all fake, but you can't, because you don't want to mess up their dreams.

When I started, I was just this husky guy who knew a little martial arts and didn't want to work in a lumberyard all his life. I jumped at the chance to be a pro wrestler. Back then, all that losing bugged me a lot. Back then, I worried girls would think I was a loser.

Then one day I realized, the hell with that, if they're so dumb they think it's real I don't want anything to do with them. So I became a jobber, and I do six or seven matches a month, and, with what Sue makes, we have enough to get by.

They aired one of my matches that weekend, and I watched it at home with Sue. They showed the match with the Barristers, and when I took that double clothesline, I took a really poor bump. Even Sue knew it.

"You were falling down before they even touched you," she said. "If they ever did touch you, that is."

I looked into her big blue eyes and told her how Lou said I'd done such a good job of selling it.

She crinkled up her nose and got up for more beers. From the kitchen she said, "You've got to get away from Lou. Find your-self another outfit to work with."

"There's not a whole lot of call for jobbers, Hon," I said. "You go where the work is. That's with Lou."

She came back in and sat on my lap and kissed my nose. Then she downed some of her beer and said, "Let's not worry about it now," and she put her head on my shoulder and got all content like she does. But a minute later wrestling was over and *Gilligan's Island* came on, and I jumped up to turn it off—the clicker was broken—and I dumped her on the sofa. Because I really hate that show.

I didn't tell Sue what Lou had said about a push. I figured I'd let it be a surprise when—if—it happened.

In Springfield the next week they had Tommy Bufone and me against the Barrister Brothers again. But the Brothers had turned babyface in the meantime. Lou was short of good-guy tag teams, so he changed their name to Pro Bono and turned them by having them bounce their manager, Sammy the Muskrat Deegan, around the ring after he lost them a match by interference against Frick and Frack, a couple of jobbers-to-the-stars. So now Tommy and I had to act mean when we were announced, making faces at the crowd and all, then Pearl-Harboring Pro Bono while they were taking their jackets off. Of course, it didn't do any good. Tommy got pinned, and I got knocked out of the ring when I went to rescue him. I sold that bump pretty damn well, if I do say so myself.

I was scheduled for one more match that day, against Man Mountain Beazel, and since he was a heel I changed into my good-guy tights. Then I watched the next match on the monitor. It was Lenny Lemaire against Thumper. Lenny would do stuff

like call himself Larry Levine in New York, or Luis Larriva anywhere there were a lot of Mexicans, but that night he was using
his real name.

After a couple of minutes Thumper put the Thump on Lenny,
and the crowd went wild. They were shaking the dressing room,
they were so worked up. I mean, this Thumper guy was over. I'd
heard they were setting him up to challenge Beast Benton for the
title, and right then I knew it was true. Beast had held the belt for
a month, since he'd won it from Terry Casino by using what they
liked to call a foreign object, and Lou never liked to let a heel be
champ too long.

The monitor showed them carting Lenny out, and Thumper
went with him. Everybody but me was watching Thumper. I was
watching Lenny. He wasn't moving at all. Then they did the bit
where Thumper runs back to the ring, and Lenny went off camera,
but just before he did I saw a guy in the corner of the screen
opening a door. It wasn't the door to the dressing room. It led
somewhere under the stands.

I slipped out into the corridor, and after a bit found myself in a
dark hallway that smelled like old beer. Somebody opened a door
that led outside, and I could see someone else sling something
over his shoulder. It was Lenny. They threw him in the trunk of
a car and slammed the lid. The guy walked back in, and Lou was
right behind him. Somebody's headlights shone in through the
door, and there I was right in the beam. Lou saw me. He put his
hands out in front of him and made a pushing motion, then
disappeared into the dark.

I found my way back to the dressing room, and there was
Thumper. I'd never seen him up close before. He must've been
six foot six. Real buff. Nowhere near the 380 pounds they
announced him at, but a solid 300 at least. He was still wearing

his outfit, the furry white tights and boots, and he had the damn rabbit ears on his head. His face was real pink, one of those faces that looked like he never had to shave.

He saw me and smiled. "Hey, little buddy," he said, just like the Skipper on *Gilligan's Island*. Now, I'm not usually anyone's little buddy. I'm six-three and 235. So I especially hated when he called me that. "Didja see me Thump?"

I drifted over to the massage table and got it between me and him. "On the monitor."

"I like to Thump," he said. "Course, sometimes I Thump a little too hard. I used to hate to do that, but now I'm gettin' to kind of like it. 'Cause the fans like it. And Lou, he likes it a lot, too, and Lou says if I keep Thumpin' I might just get to be champ someday."

He pulled off his boots and stripped off his tights and laid them real careful into an army green duffel bag. Then he said, "Better watch out, little buddy. I might just have to Thump you sometime." He grinned, but the grin was all around his mouth. His eyes were little pig eyes in that pink bunny face.

Still wearing his ears, he went off toward the showers. "Don't call me 'little buddy,'" I said.

A week later Lou called. "I'm calling about your push," he said. "I haven't figured out all the angles yet, but I just wanted you to know it's still coming."

"That's good, Lou."

He gave this funny high laugh. "Did you see Thumper on TV the other day?"

"I must have missed it."

"Best thing that's happened to this federation in a long, long time."

"Yeah," I said. "Speaking of Thumper, I haven't seen Lenny Lemaire lately."

It was only a second before he said, "Didn't you hear? His mother's real sick, and he's gone back to Alabama to take care of her."

"That's a damn shame," I said.

"That it is." Lou cleared his throat. "Now, we've got a card coming up in Easton . . ."

"Uh-huh."

"You'll job there, but by the next taping I think I'll have a big surprise ready for you."

"That'll be great, Lou," I said. "I like surprises."

Easton was on a Friday night. It was a house card, which meant most of the matches didn't have jobbers in them but instead had heel stars against face stars. There were only two jobbers in the dressing room. I was scheduled to go against Monster Madigan, and Paul Tompkins was up against Thumper.

Paul wore black tights and a mask with big white felt teeth and went on as The Shark. Sometimes we'd be a tag team together, and they let me wear the same getup, and we were The Sharks. I never got around to making a mask with teeth and would always have to scotch tape some on at the last minute. When we were The Sharks, Lou would let us do a little better, actually pound our opponents for a little while, with me getting in some martial arts stuff, before one of us ended on our back—one, two, three.

I found Paul sitting in a corner of the dressing room. He was real sweaty already, even though they had the air conditioning on way high. He filled his cheeks with air and blew it out slow. "You know much about Thumper?"

"Enough," I said.

"Nobody knows his real name," he said. "No one's even sure where he came from."

"Lou must know."

The Michigan Men ambled into the dressing room. They'd just been beaten by Pro Bono. They were laughing and talking about some girl in Cleveland.

"I'm up," Paul said.

"Do good."

He nodded and pulled on his Shark mask and walked through the curtain into the arena. I sat down by the monitor. Funny things, those monitors. During the parts of the show when the folks at home see all the commercials, the monitors still show what's going on ringside. So I watched Paul walk down the aisle, past all the fans who didn't know him from Adam, and on past the broadcasting booth.

Something happened there I'm sure no one but me saw. As Paul walked by the booth, he turned in Joe and Lou's direction. And Lou put his hands out in front of him and gave a little push. After that, Paul walked to the ring a little faster and a little straighter. The thing is, he didn't walk out of it again.

Later I was sitting in the dark in my motel room. I'd just told the guy at the desk to give me a wakeup call at six. That way I'd be home to Sue by one or so the next afternoon. Since it was Saturday, we could have most of the day together.

I was rubbing my right knee, which I'd bruised during my three and a half minutes in the ring with Monster Madigan, thinking about finding some ice to pack around it. Somebody knocked on the door. "It's Lou."

I slowly walked to the door and pulled it open. "It's late, Lou."

"I'll just be a minute."

He came in. He had on that damn raincoat. His eyes scanned the place. "Kind of a pit," he said.

"It's a jobber room."

He nodded and sat on one of the rickety wooden chairs. "Once you get your push, you'll be able to afford better than this."

"And that'll be . . ."

"Next week, at the taping in Grandville. We're going to call you Samson Sanders. You'll come out in this strongman getup."

"Face or heel?"

"I'm not sure yet. Probably face. I've got a couple of contract negotiations in the next few days, and I have to see what the balance is after that."

I couldn't help myself. This big stupid smile grew on my face.

"There's just one thing," Lou said.

The stupid smile went back where it belonged. "What's that?"

"Nothing much," he said. "I just need you to job once more. It'll be early in the card. The crowd won't even remember you by the time Samson Sanders shows up." He got up and walked out without saying another word.

I got undressed and into bed. I had the radio on low, because sometimes that helps me fall asleep. A Tom Petty song came on, and that's when I remembered Lenny Lemaire didn't come from Alabama. He always used to sing that song. "Louisiana Rain," it was called.

The get-up came by UPS a couple of days later. This fake fur loincloth thing, leather arm and leg bands, and the dumbest wig I'd ever seen. Sue saw it and got a laughing fit. I put it on, and soon she was rolling on the floor laughing. Then I went into a muscleman pose, and she pulled me down on top of her. I kept the wig on while we did it.

*   *   *

The TV taping was the next Saturday. I let Sue sleep and slipped out before seven. I drove slow and careful and still got to the arena with two hours to spare.

I put on my new outfit, checked it out in the crummy old mirror, and put it away. I sat there in my underwear for a little while, then put on my bad-guy tights. I just had a feeling I was going to be the heel in that jobber match.

Joe wandered into the dressing room with the card. Seventeen matches, enough to feed the TV audience for weeks, enough to keep the arena crowd happy even if most of the matches were squashes. I started at the bottom and looked for Samson Sanders. He wasn't there. I kept scanning until I got to the first match on the card. There was my name. My real name.

Across from it was Thumper.

The rest of the gang began to trickle in. Everyone but Thumper. At three o'clock somebody stuck his head in and called me to the ring. I zipped up my bag and tossed it on the floor and slowly walked out of the dressing room, then down that long walkway. The place was only about half full, though lots of folks were still streaming in. As I passed the broadcast booth I thought of looking for Lou, then said the hell with it. If he was giving me that damn push sign I didn't want to know about it.

The ring announcer introed me, and I did my heel gig, throwing my fists up in the air, beating my chest, howling at the one or two people who'd noticed me.

The announcer drew in a deep breath. "Ladies and gentlemen," he said, "His opponent, weighing in at three hundred and ninety pounds, from Green Meadow, Nebraska . . . Thump—per!"

He came marching down the aisle, looking more pumped than ever, getting a huge pop from the crowd. They yelled. They screamed. Ladies blew kisses. Men held up their kids.

He came down to ringside, wearing that big Green Meadow smile, the one that stopped somewhere around his nose. He hopped up the metal steps and stepped over all three ring ropes. He glared at me across the ring, pointed his big finger, and shouted, "You're going down, little buddy!"

I said, "Don't call me that." He just laughed.

We started with a collar-and-elbow tie-up. He tossed me away. As the heel, it was up to me to make the first illegal move. Once I did that, he could pound me, and finally Thump me. I locked up with him a couple more times, letting him throw me all the way out of the ring after the last one. I complained to the ref about a hair pull, and he rambled over to Thumper like they always do and told him not to do it again. We tangled again, and I came out of it with my left arm in a wringer.

It was about time to elbow him in the face. I put a little more into it than I had to to sell it, and he got a little surprised expression. Not enough so the crowd would notice. He kicked me in the stomach, and I went down. I got up a little faster than he expected. He threw a couple of lefts, a couple of rights, and I went down again. He body-slammed me and dragged me up by my hair, suplexed me, and pulled me up again. Then he threw me over his shoulder.

"This is it, little buddy," he whispered. "Thumpin' time." He ran forward and started to twist me around so my face would smash the mat.

It was the little buddy stuff that did it.

I broke his neck.

It's easy when you know how. When you've had the right kind of martial arts. While he was tossing me around his head, I just threw out a hand, and then the other, and grabbed and twisted.

Nobody in the crowd saw anything except me trying to catch onto something. And they were yelling so loud none of them heard the crack.

I sold the rest of the move and hit the mat just in time to have Thumper come crashing down on top of me. I managed to get both my shoulders down before he hit me like a big sack of cement. Right then, he really did feel like the 380 or 390 or whatever they were saying that week.

The ref didn't know what to do. "Count," I whispered. He finally did—one, two, three, and there it was, Thumper had won. Just like he was supposed to.

And that's what really counts, isn't it?

Nathan Walpow is the author of the Joe Portugal series of mystery novels, including The Cactus Club Killings *and* Death of an Orchid Lover. *This is his first short crime fiction. Nathan is a former actor and a five-times-undefeated* Jeopardy! *champion. He welcomes email to nathan@walpow.com and website visits at http://walpow.com.*

FATAL TEARS

Ekaterine Nikas

Murder is not usually an activity contemplated when the sun beats hot and the sky shines blue. But when I entered the kitchen that warm August afternoon and smelled the fresh-baked scones Mrs. Halliwell always made for Sunday afternoon tea, I felt a trembling in my stomach that had nothing whatsoever to do with hunger.

This was to be the day.

I crossed to the door of the small walk-in closet where at least three starched white aprons always hung ready for use and slowly slipped one on, willing the weakness in my arms and legs to go away. It didn't.

Fortunately, there was no one to notice my lack of composure. Mrs. Halliwell always took Sundays off after she finished the morning baking, and my adopted sister, Alex, never set a well-heeled foot in the kitchen. Hoping to bury my nervousness in ritual, I began laying out the tea things as I had every Sunday as far back as I could remember.

My Sunday afternoon teas with Alex had begun when I was

twelve. Alex had just entered law school and was gliding through the rigors of her first year with the same dispiriting ease with which she managed every task. Our parents were away, as they almost always were, and Alex had decided it was her duty to take me in hand.

At first, I'd been touched by her interest, for Alex—with her honey-brown skin and silver-gold hair and perfect, unshakeable poise—had far worthier claims on her attention than an awkward teenage sister with a freckled nose and two left feet. However, sharing warm moments over tea and scones was not exactly what Alex had in mind. Mild inquiries about my week soon turned to grim interrogations, and I quickly learned that any pleasure I'd chance to encounter while out of Alex's presence would be wrung out and squeezed dry at our Sunday meetings. Even after our parents' death on a snowy Swiss road, she had kept up the ritual with oppressive regularity, until now I hated our Sunday afternoon teas almost as much as I hated Alex.

I gathered up dishes, napkins, linen, and silverware and carefully arranged them on the black lacquered tray I used to carry everything to the conservatory. Then I began to arrange the imported tea biscuits Alex always insisted upon onto a plate. The process was oddly soothing. Each soft thud of a biscuit clinking against the fine china sounded like the echo of my heart.

Suddenly the comforting quiet of the kitchen was broken by the scream of the teakettle. I had been too focused on what I was doing to notice the warning snufflings as the water neared its boil. Now the fierce shriek felt like a blow. I jerked backwards, knocking both cups off the tray and onto the floor with a crash. *Clumsy, Dee, very clumsy.* Alex's familiar taunt trembled in the air like a ghostly whisper. Only Alex wasn't a ghost—yet. I stumbled to the stove and lifted the screeching kettle off the burner.

Suddenly there wasn't enough air in the entire kitchen to satisfy my bursting lungs.

I sank to my knees, struggling for breath, and kept my eyes fixed on the swinging door to the kitchen, expecting Alex's tall figure to appear at any moment to survey the chaos. I knew her arrival would mark an end to my scheme. One chillingly disdainful look from beneath those perfectly arched brows would be enough to freeze my determination to act, perhaps forever.

But Alex did not come.

My breathing slowed and steadied, and my heart ceased its frantic pounding. I rose to my feet. I poured the still steaming water into the teapot and added the tea ball filled with Alex's favorite blend of Darjeeling. Then I fetched the broom and dustpan, cleaned up the broken crockery, took out two new cups from the cupboard and carefully placed them on the tray with fingers that no longer shook.

Marking my cup with a large crumb in the saucer, I reached into my pocket and withdrew the small, brown vial I had received in the mail from Amicus. I twisted off the black cap to reveal the built-in dropper. Amicus had said the liquid inside the vial was colorless, odorless, tasteless—and very powerful. I would need only two drops.

Even at that it would be risky. Alex always insisted on pouring her tea herself. I would have to place the drops in her empty cup and hope she didn't notice them before she poured her tea. Still, it was worth the risk. Alex was the obstacle that stood between me and my best—and perhaps last—chance at happiness. Gently I squeezed the black bulb of the dropper and watched as two glistening drops of poison slid like fatal tears into the delicate Royal Doulton cup.

*   *   *

The conservatory had changed little since I was a child, unlike the rest of the house, which my mother had relentlessly redecorated every year until her death. I suspect Alex would have been happy to continue the tradition, except for the fact that the house was now technically mine, my father having been unwilling to leave it to anyone but a Wheaton by blood. Still, that didn't stop Alex from rearranging things endlessly. As far as she was concerned, the house was still her home. Legally I could have thrown her out. In reality, however, I could no more eject her from my household than I could free myself from her control over every aspect of my life.

"You're twenty minutes late," she greeted me as I entered the light, plant-filled room.

"Sorry," I murmured as I set the tray down on the pretty glass-topped table I had loved spinning as a child until Alex had caught me at it. I slid the placemats, napkins, cups and saucers into place with well-practiced efficiency, then set the teapot, biscuits, and Mrs. Halliwell's scones down in the center of the table. I finished with the silverware and then sat down, eyeing Alex's intent expression uneasily.

"Will you pour?" I asked, the question rhetorical. But my eagerness to have her do just that was screaming in my head.

She nodded slowly, her ice blue eyes and carefully outlined mouth narrowed in an expression that reminded me of some beautiful yet dangerous bird of prey. Still, I was grateful her gaze was fixed on me and not the china. All the way from the kitchen I had stared at the wet sheen in her cup, wondering how I would convince the meticulous Alex to use china she might think soiled.

With her eyes still fixed on my face, she began to reach for the handle of the teapot, then stopped.

I swallowed, hard.

"Deidre," she said, her hand retreating to her lap, "There's something we need to discuss."

"There is?" I squeaked, my voice high and tense. I took a deep breath and forced my voice lower, my tone calmer. "Well, can't we discuss it over our tea? I've already kept you waiting."

For a moment, a puzzled frown flitted across her face; then her expression changed, lightened, and became amused. She glanced at the teapot, and I held my breath. Her gaze flicked from the teapot down to her cup and then up to my face again. "Drop the crockery again?" she said in a tone an outsider would probably have considered mildly teasing. I winced. "Never mind. I think we'll both enjoy our tea more after we've talked this through."

"Very well," I said. "What's bothering you?"

She gazed at me for a long time, stretching out the silence until it was thick enough to slice. She might not be a Wheaton by birth, but she had all our father's sense of the dramatic. She also had a lawyer's flair for using pauses to intimidate. Yet when she spoke, her voice was almost gentle.

"I understand Jim Trent is back in town."

Nothing she could have said would have caught me more off balance. I felt betraying heat rise in my cheeks. Jim Trent was the man I had planned to marry until he'd disappeared without a word three months earlier.

"Why should that mean anything to me?" I replied, trying to sound indifferent, despite the fact that until the day before yesterday I'd had a habit of jerking around with an odd pain in my chest whenever I'd seen a beat-up Ford pick-up drive by.

"Please, Deidre," Alex said, "I know we've had our differences, but can't we talk honestly for once? I may only be your adopted sister, but that doesn't mean I don't care about you." Her voice was full of such solicitude that for a moment I had a sick feeling in my stomach, remembering the poison waiting in her cup. Then I reminded myself that this was Alex, master of the credible lie. For some reason, she was putting on an act of sisterly concern, but that didn't mean it was real.

"I see," I said. "You care about me. Is that why you wrote Jim a check for fifty thousand dollars and told him to head for the Caribbean and stay there?"

Alex bowed her head in an apparent gesture of remorse. My stomach lurched again, but my mouth tightened. Alex never felt remorse. Besides, Jim was not the first. Over the years I'd grown used to Alex waving her checkbook or her body at any man who showed an interest in me. And in the end she hadn't had to write all that many checks. A small redhead with hazel eyes and an average figure was hardly a match for Alex.

"I'm sorry, Dee," Alex said. "You were so infatuated with him I thought you couldn't see straight. Men like Jim don't usually fall for women like you." She paused. "I was sure he was just another fortune-hunting bastard after the Wheaton millions."

Her words hurt, but I had so much emotion churning inside me, I hardly noticed. "You forget, Alex, I was planning to marry Jim. He was going to get my millions. So what did you say to him that made him settle for fifty thousand instead?"

Our eyes locked. Reluctantly she said, "I made it clear that as your trustee I hold the purse strings until you're thirty. I told him that if you were foolish enough to marry him, I'd cut off your allowance, and the two of you would have to make do for the next eight years on what he makes selling his paintings."

"I see," I said. Jim had told me as much. He'd also told me that Alex's threats had never mattered to him, that the money had never mattered either. It had been his anger at me after our last fight that had driven him to take Alex's check. It had been a mistake, he said, which is why he had come back. Now it was up to me to decide if money was going to keep us apart.

Unfortunately, Jim didn't seem to realize that it wasn't money that was most likely to come between us.

It was Alex.

She caught my look and her expression turned entreating. "Please, Dee, I did what I thought was right. I figured that if I faced him with that kind of choice, he'd settle for the quick score, take the money I offered him, and run."

"You were wrong." The words came out an angry whisper.

"Yes, I was," she agreed, her voice almost apologetic. I felt my jaw sag in disbelief. Alex never admitted she was wrong. "You see," she continued, "he never cashed my check."

"I know," I murmured distractedly, still stunned by her admission of fallibility.

"I thought you might," she said, flashing me an intent look. Too late, I realized what I had admitted. "He came to see you Friday, didn't he?"

I nodded, my hands clenched tightly in my lap.

"You needn't look like that, Dee," she said, cocking her head at a slight angle that reminded me suddenly of our mother. "I'm not going to scold you."

Unexpected tears pricked at the corners of my eyes. Alex had made my life hell as far back as I could remember, yet it suddenly occurred to me that when she was gone I would be utterly, completely alone.

"I just want to know if congratulations are in order."

"What?" I exclaimed, startled out of my reverie.

"I just want to know if you two are planning to get married now," Alex said, her voice rueful, "because if you are, I wanted to assure you I have no intention of stopping your allowance or doing anything to get in the way of your happiness."

I stared at her. There had to be a catch—somewhere. Hoping to surprise a more honest reaction out of her, I said, "Actually, we've already applied for the license."

Her expression remained serene. "Do you want me to phone Dr. Mackenzie's office to make an appointment for the blood tests?"

Slowly, my thoughts frozen in confusion, I shook my head. "Jim took care of it through his doctor. We went to the hospital lab and had it done there."

"Community General?" Alex inquired tranquilly.

I nodded, suddenly desperate to shake her ever-perfect poise. "We plan to get married tomorrow."

But all she did was ask softly, "Am I invited?"

I clamped my teeth together and fought off the urge to scream. "You don't really expect me to believe you're going to just sit back and let me bring Jim into this house as my husband without a fight?"

An odd look came over Alex's face. "I don't know why not," she said, "it's your home after all, not mine." She picked up the teapot and poured tea into both our cups. My heart began to race. She raised her cup to her lips.

And stopped.

She set the cup down again. "It seems I've forgotten something." She looked at the table. "And so, by the look of things, have you, Dee."

Anxiously I scanned the table. Then I realized my mistake. Alex's honey pot. I'd forgotten it. She never drank her Darjeeling without honey. It was an odd taste, but not one I could afford to buck now. "I'll get it," I told her and hurried from the room. As I walked along, an image of her face as she'd said, "It's your home after all, not mine," lingered in my mind.

Alex was a very successful lawyer, and every investment she touched seemed to turn to gold. I doubted she was hurting financially. Yet for the first time, I considered that I was not the only one to suffer from my parents' ill-conceived will.

I had often wished my parents had left their money differently, that Alex, not I, had received the lion's share of our parents' fortune, and that I had been left the small but unrestricted portion that had been Alex's inheritance. Millions in the bank don't mean much when you've no access to them and every move you make is monitored.

But my parents, though they had held Alex in high regard for her beauty and style and passion for money, had in the end decided an adopted daughter was not quite good enough to be the heir. Until that moment, I'd never considered what it must have been like for Alex to be passed over like that simply because the right blood didn't flow in her veins. I suddenly could imagine all too clearly why she had always been so hostile to me. I had displaced her. Not as a younger child displaces a firstborn, but as a true heir displaces a pretender to the throne. In my parents' eyes, an adopted child would always be second best.

By the time I reached the kitchen I was panting. Such insights are not helpful when you are about to commit murder. Until that moment I had felt myself justified to use any means possible to free myself of Alex's tyranny. But now I'd made the mistake of realizing that Alex, too, was a victim of my parents' folly. How can one victim justifiably kill another?

I crossed to the walk-in cupboard and withdrew the honey pot.

Victim. I thought of the angry confrontation I'd had with Jim the day he had disappeared from my life three months ago, when he'd accused me of hiding behind that word to avoid life. He'd argued then that while I claimed I wanted to be free of Alex, everything I did, said, and thought was controlled by her.

I suddenly realized that he was right.

I started back to the conservatory with dragging steps. I had thought murdering Alex would finally gain me control, but now I realized that was only an illusion. Poisoning Alex was going to become the anchor that would sink my life once and for all. Oh, God, what a mistake I'd made. I'd screwed up and there was no turning back. I feared I would enter the conservatory to find Alex slumped over the table, victorious over me even in death.

The image was so vivid that when I entered the room to find Alex not only conscious but surveying me with bright, amused eyes, I almost stumbled. "H-here's the honey," I said.

"So I see. I'm glad it didn't end up on the floor."

The mockery in her tone braced me. It was a reminder that if I really meant to start conducting my life differently, I would have to begin now. I gazed down at my cup, at the crumb on the saucer that proclaimed my safety and Alex's danger. I was responsible for the poison in Alex's tea; now it was up to me to see she didn't drink it.

I set the honey down on the table. Alex picked up the dripper and began twirling it slowly over her cup, sending a golden thread cascading into the Darjeeling's dark depths. She caught me watching her. "You act like you've never seen a woman add honey to her tea before," she said.

"That tea must be practically cold by now. Why don't I go back to the kitchen and make us a new batch?"

"Nonsense," Alex said, wrapping one long, thin hand around her cup. "It's just the right temperature. You know that teapot keeps it nice and hot." Once more, she began to raise her cup to her lips.

I sat there, wondering if I should scream, yell, upend the whole table to stop her. I was poised ready to slap the cup out of her hand, when deliverance came in the form of a slight buzzing.

It was Alex's cellular phone. Annoyance flickered across her face; then she set down her cup and rose to her feet. "Excuse me," she said brusquely, as she extracted the phone from the breast pocket of her well-tailored suit, turned her back on me, and headed for the far corner of the room.

As I watched her tense back and listened to the angry mutter of her voice into the telephone, I realized this was my chance. I gazed down at the glass table with its spinning top. I would have to turn it slowly, so as not to slop the tea, but it could be done, allowing me to switch the cups without ever leaving my seat.

There was only one hitch. Alex was standing near a mirror. From time to time she cast brief glances at it, and since I could see her face when she did it, no doubt she could also see me.

I picked up the dripper and added honey to my own tea, trying to match the amount Alex had put in hers. When I'd finished, I set the dripper back in the pot and waited. I calculated it would take a count of five to turn the table. I began counting to see how long Alex took between glances. They were too close together. I wouldn't be able to turn the table in that short a time.

Suddenly I realized Alex was watching me. Thinking it would look more natural if I was drinking my tea, I raised my cup to my lips. Then someone on the other end of the line gave Alex some news that made her swear. She moved slightly, apparently for more privacy, and as she did so, she turned away from the mirror. I didn't wait. I set down my untouched cup and began rotating the table, glad to note the cups and place settings looked identical.

I had almost gotten it all the way around when Alex moved again. I stopped, my heart in my throat, as she flicked another glance at the mirror. I sat very still, hoping she wouldn't notice the altered orientation of the table. Apparently she didn't, for her glance flicked away again.

I hurriedly finished turning the table the rest of the way.

The safe cup, the one with the crumb in the saucer, was now in front of Alex's place, and the poisoned tea sat in front of me.

Alex slammed the antenna down, shoved the phone back into her pocket, and stalked back to the table. I could see her working to calm herself. After a few deep breaths, she sat down again.

"Business?" I inquired politely.

"Of a sort," she snapped, her irritation still obvious.

I nodded agreeably. Having successfully switched the cups, I was in a forgiving mood.

Alex picked up her tea and took a sip. She took several more, before looking my way and noticing I wasn't joining her. Her well-shaped eyebrows lifted in reproof.

"Come on, Dee, you're the one who was telling me not to let the tea get cold. Drink up."

I stared down at the cup in front of me. Death shimmered in its tepid depths. "Somehow I'm not in the mood anymore," I said as lightly as I could.

"That's too bad," Alex said, downing her own tea and then setting her cup carefully on the table. "It would be such a shame to see all that good Darjeeling go to waste." There was an edge to her voice that should have set off alarm bells in my head. Unfortunately, I just assumed she was still angry from her call.

She reached into another pocket of her jacket and withdrew something small, sleek, and shiny. I stared at it for several seconds before my dazed mind accepted that it was a gun.

As she lifted the gun and pointed it directly at me, Alex's finger curled around the trigger in a gesture that was almost a caress.

"I'm sorry, Deidre, but I'm afraid I'm going to have to insist you drink your tea."

I stared at her. "You can't be serious, Alex!"

"Oh, but I am. Deadly serious."

"But you can't shoot me! You'd be arrested for murder."

"Not murder," Alex said calmly. "Self-defense." She extracted an envelope from yet another pocket with her free hand and tossed it across the table to me.

Slowly, with clumsy fingers, I removed the contents of the envelope. A cut-out newspaper ad spilled out, as did several type-written pages that looked disturbingly familiar.

A heaviness settled over me as I recognized the ad. *Is there an obstacle standing between you and your dreams?* the familiar words read. *Don't give up. I can help you.* As I gazed at the words that had once echoed in my head like a whispered promise, I felt a growing sense of dread.

She knew. My brain fumbled to understand how it could be so, but Alex knew.

I picked up the first of the typewritten sheets and unfolded it. I had been right in thinking it familiar. It was my initial reply to the ad, addressed to Amicus, and it contained my first oblique reference to murder. *My obstacle has a name,* I had written. *Can you help me?*

Amicus had—for a price—by supplying me with the tasteless, colorless poison I had thought would finally set me free. What folly. I looked up into Alex's now openly malevolent face. I had to face facts. There was only one way she could have gotten those letters.

"It was you, wasn't it?" I asked. "You all the time. You were Amicus."

Her ice blue eyes suddenly looked colder than I had ever seen them.

"Yes."

When I'd answered that ad, I'd thought I was striking out, breaking free, taking my destiny in my own hands. Instead, I'd merely been acting as Alex's puppet, performing on cue like one of Pavlov's well-trained dogs. Humiliation overwhelmed me as I uttered a single strangled word, "*Why?*"

"I wanted to kill you, of course," Alex replied, "but I knew as your heir I'd be the prime suspect. I decided that if I could stage it so that you were plotting to murder me, I could convince the police that you had accidentally ingested your own poison."

"But how could you know I'd even see the ad or reply to it?"

Alex shrugged. "You were always boringly predictable, Dee. I placed the ad in the one paper I knew you read cover to cover—that counter-culture rag you're always sneaking in when you think I don't notice. Then I filled the ad with the sort of childish nonsense I knew you'd find appealing, choosing the name Amicus because it sounded gothic enough to intrigue you."

"And this was all about the money?" I said, flabbergasted at how dangerously oblivious I'd been to Alex's ambitions.

"Of course."

"But I don't understand your timing. Mother and Father died three years ago. If you were so determined to kill me for their fortune, why the hell did you wait until now?"

Her eyes locked with mine. "Since the crash of their Ferrari wasn't the accident it appeared to be, I thought it wise to allow sufficient time to pass before doing away with you as well."

I stared at her, fighting down the bile that threatened to rise up my throat. "Are you trying to tell me that—"

"Come, Dee. We both know that as parents they—to put it bluntly—sucked. It did no great harm to dispose of them."

"But—"

"As far as the timing of your own demise, I'd planned to allow you another year. However, I've had some bad investments recently that necessitate a large and quick infusion of capital."

It finally sank in that Alex truly meant to kill me. "You won't get away with it," I said shakily, the words unconvincing even to my own ears. "Jim is bound to ask questions."

"He might, at that. Fortunately, he isn't going to live long enough to ask about tomorrow's paper, let alone your untimely passing. You recall my earlier phone call? That was one of the gentlemen I've hired to take care of his removal for me."

My skin went cold. "Alex, no! There's no need to hurt Jim! He won't make waves. He doesn't even care about me anymore. I made that up about our getting married just to upset you."

She flashed me a mocking smile. "Nice try, Dee, but you never were a very good liar."

"Alex, please. Leave Jim alone. He's nothing to you."

"On the contrary, Dee. His unexpected return has put a rather large crimp in my plans. You see, the motive I was going to give the police for your trying to kill me was anger that I'd driven him away. His reappearance and your subsequent plans to marry undermine the credibility of that story. Which is why he has to be eliminated, as does all record of his return from parts unknown."

"But you can't eliminate all record of it!" I exclaimed. "It's impossible! There's the license, the blood tests—"

"Nothing is impossible with money, Dee. You never did learn that lesson. I've already arranged for the license to be misfiled— permanently. As for the blood tests . . . well, you were a big help with that. I wasn't sure where you'd had them performed, but now that I know, I can see that they, too, are made to disappear."

"Alex, I beg you! Jim doesn't matter. Those letters are proof enough of what I intended. You can tell the police anything you want about why I wanted to kill you. They'll believe you."

Alex's thin eyebrows rose. "Really, Dee, show some pride. Groveling isn't going to help this time, you know."

Something snapped inside me. Anger, white-hot and as fortifying as tempered steel, shot through my veins. "Alex, I don't think you're thinking this through clearly."

Alex's pink-frosted lips tightened. "Is that so?"

"If you're trying to avoid questions from the police, then shooting me is a big mistake. It would look a lot less suspicious if I just drank this tea. Of course, I don't have any reason to be that cooperative, unless . . ." I let my voice trail away.

"Unless?" she demanded sharply.

"Unless you give me your word that Jim walks away from this alive."

For a moment, Alex hesitated, then slowly she nodded. She took out her phone and dialed a number. After a few moments she said, "Cancel the job. Leave Trent alone. He's no longer an issue." Then she hung up.

She looked at me expectantly. "Well?"

I looked down at my cup of tea. Slowly I lifted it to my lips. Then I downed it in one gulp.

Alex relaxed visibly. "Good girl." She set the gun down on the table but kept it within easy reach.

"You'll keep your word about Jim?"

"Of course, my dear, word of a Wheaton." Her voice was silky, and I knew that she lied. I'd bought Jim some time, nothing more.

I wanted to scream and rage, but the thought of my impending death and Jim's, too, was too overwhelming to grasp. A fatalistic calm settled over me.

"Weren't you taking a considerable risk," I asked, "sending me the poison instead of just promising it to me? I suppose you wanted me to handle the vial and get my fingerprints on it, but didn't you worry I might slip you the poison when you weren't expecting it?"

Alex's lips curled in amusement. "To be honest, Dee, I never thought you'd have the guts to try to poison me. In fact, when I saw those drops in my cup I almost felt proud of you. But I'm not crazy. I wasn't about to take a chance and send you real poison. What I sent in the mail was a perfectly harmless homeopathic concoction I got at the health food store."

"But . . ." I began, and then stopped, biting my lip. Sudden hope flared in my chest, but I knew my life might depend on keeping that hope out of my face. I forced myself to frown.

"Don't look so worried, my dear," said Alex soothingly. "The gentleman who supplied me with the real poison—which I placed in your cup while you were so helpfully fetching the honey—assures me it is quite painless and almost symptomless until the end." She looked down at her watch. "He also assures me it is very quick. It usually acts in less than five min—"

She stopped abruptly, a sudden panicked look appearing in her eyes. "Deidre . . ." My name came out a rasping gurgle. "Why were you so reluctant to drink your tea?"

I looked her straight in the eye. "I switched the cups while you were on the phone. I'd decided, you see, that I didn't want to kill you after all. Ironic, isn't it, that at the end your puppet cut her strings?"

She stared at me, her face suddenly drained of all color, and then her hand dropped convulsively toward the gun. I was ready for her. I spun the table, and the gun went flying onto the floor. For a moment, I thought she was going to make a dive for it, but then she began to sway.

"I should have known," she whispered. "You've been *my* obstacle, my nemesis, since the day you were born." The words rattled in her throat, and then she pitched forward onto the table with an odd little gasp. By the time I reached her, she was dead, the shattered pieces of her cup scattered around her head like a distorted halo. While I waited for the police to come, I picked up one of the shards and ran its jagged edge against my finger, shakily pondering one of Alex's favorite quotes: *Whatever does not destroy me makes me stronger.*

Her death was ruled a suicide. The vial with the real poison was found in her pocket with only Alex's fingerprints on it, and the news that she was almost bankrupt supplied a plausible motive.

After the ruling was announced, I rose from my seat and took Jim's arm. We walked out slowly to face the hordes of cameras and reporters waiting for me to comment on the lurid circumstances of my sister's death. For the most part, Jim managed to brush them away with a growled "No comment." But one reporter persevered and shoved a microphone into my face, demanding to know how I felt about Alex's suicide. For a moment, my fingers tightened around the china shard I carried in my pocket, then taking a deep breath, I lifted my head and said in a somber, trembling voice that played very well on the evening news, "I'm just sad, that's all. Very, very sad."

Which perhaps goes to show that I'm not such a bad liar after all.

Ekaterine Nikas has authored several electronic textbooks for the California State University Consortium. She has won numerous awards for her fiction writing, including the 1999 Karen Besecker

Memorial Award for best novice mystery writer and Best of Show across all genres in the 1998 Authorlink! New Author Awards. She is currently working on her third novel, a suspense story about a universal codebreaker and the search for a missing mathematician. To learn more about her work, please visit her website at:

http://home.earthlink.net/~ktnikas/index.html.

MISS PARKER & THE CUTTER-SANBORN TABLES

Gay Toltl Kinman

The week of Halloween started when Miss Parker was found, head and arms on her desk, a foot-long Civil War sword through her body.

No question about her being dead; the blood, the smashed lamp, and the mess on her desk told all.

She lay stiff and cold all weekend, an apt description of her in life, not that anyone, including me, voiced that to the police.

Miss Parker's Civil War sword, actually a replica, complete with pearl handle and tassled hilt, had been used to stab her in the back. The irony was not lost on those of us in library school, particularly those of us in her cataloging class. Back-stabbing was something Miss Parker was good at. But, we had to agree, she wasn't good enough to do herself in.

The history of the sword was well-known throughout the school, as Miss Parker had often told us and anyone else who would listen, of her Civil War ancestor who had saved the life of *the* President—Jefferson Davis—with a sword. Davis, in turn, had presented a replica to the same Parker forebear. The sized-down sword was razor-sharp; Miss Parker used it for a letter opener.

Someone else had another use for it.

As we buzzed around in the halls, rumors abounded. We were curious who our next cataloging instructor would be. Justin Rampart, the assistant dean, might be tapped as her replacement. It was no secret that he was generous with high grades for the men in his class. Not that I would be any worse off; Miss Parker only gave one A per class, and Justin Rampart rarely failed anyone.

"Maiden lady," said my roommate, Hsing, with a respectful note in her voice, "is no more." She leaned against the hallway wall.

I nodded. The feared Miss Parker definitely was no more, along with her stories about her Virginia antecedents and The War of Northern Aggression, as she called it.

"And no more Cuttering," Hsing said.

Cuttering was libraryese for a person's name in the Cutter-Sanborn Tables. In essence, it was a way of cataloging last names. The list gave the first letter and a two or three-digit number for the author's name, resulting in an alpha-numeric code called the book number.

In her attempt at furthering our cataloguing expertise, Miss Parker Cuttered the names of her varied and illustrious ancestors on the board during class. Every class. We all probably saw them in our sleep.

Beauregard	B432
Bouchard	B66
Kinman	K51
Lee	L477
Parker	P37
Randolph	R23

"The Cuttering of Miss Parker's ancestors and the cuttering of Miss Parker."

"Not the same, Kris," Hsing said.

"It is when I catalog," I said. "I butcher everything."

"We need more practice. Let us go to it."

I knew what she meant. We each had been given a book to catalog. I had something on petroleum. This was probably the only time in my life I hated books.

"Do you think we still have to do the assignment? She's not going to be in class tomorrow. She's dead!"

"We do it," Hsing said. Her voice was firm, so I knew I wasn't going to be able to postpone the inevitable. She started walking toward the lab where all the cataloging books were. Torture for me, heaven for Hsing.

As we walked down the hall, I saw Bernie Cunningham coming toward us. I stopped Hsing, and we watched him. He approached everyone with a large manila envelope, holding it open like a well. Even from where we stood I could read the thick, red lettering: "Flowers for Miss Parker."

"He's collecting flowers for Miss Parker's funeral?"

Hsing whispered, "He is smoking foot coverings."

"He's high on something, that's for sure. Why does he need such a large envelope?" I whispered back.

In tandem, we turned and walked the other way.

"Easier to roll water up the mountain," said Hsing, shaking her head.

"I thought he was still in the hospital."

"His term paper due," she said.

"But, surely, he could get an extension; didn't he have something like a burst appendix?"

As we rounded the corner, Hsing halted. "Kris, we find murderer."

"*You* roll water up the mountain. Why should we do that?"

Hsing pointed to a cardboard skeleton dangling above an office door.

"But that's a Halloween decoration," I said. Then she gestured at the filmy cobwebs, oversize spiders, flying witches, and other symbols I expected to see at this time of year.

"We have class at night. Campus big and black." Also big and black were Hsing's eyes as she spoke. "Person," she made stabbing motions, "still here."

Suddenly a chill pinched my spine. I shivered. She was right; we could be in danger, and I didn't see the police catching the killer right away.

"But we don't know anything about finding a murderer," I said.

"No, but we are good librarians. We do cataloguing assignment."

With that, we went into the lab and sat down at the worn wooden table where the fat, heavy *Library of Congress Subject Headings* volumes lay.

"First find classification number."

I picked up my petroleum book.

"No, Kris. Classification number for murder."

We had to find a subject heading. Next to the subject heading was the Library of Congress classification number—another cataloging system. After reviewing our options from a list in the book, we decided on "Detective," which gave us HV 8081. With that number we could go to the shelves in the stacks and find all the books on that subject.

We could have gone to the online catalog—a terminal was in the room—but Hsing insisted on doing it as Miss Parker had taught us. The old-fashioned way.

We dashed off to the bowels of the library, Hsing clutching the piece of paper with the classification number on it.

Being in the bookstacks was suddenly scary. I hadn't noticed before, but the metal flooring and shelving creaked and clicked as our shoes clunked and clattered along the low-ceilinged, narrow walkways as we headed to our destination.

We squinted in the dim light, looking for the classification number we wanted. Chilly drafts blew up between the metal plates. They sounded like someone moaning.

"Here," I said, grabbing *How To Be A Detective*. The call number was:

> HV
> 8081
> K51

"The Library of Congress classification number, together with the Cutter number, makes up the complete call number, which is unique and different for each book." Hsing gave such a perfect mimicking of Miss Parker's oft-repeated statement in her Virginia accent that I wanted to look around for her ghost.

"A for us for cataloguing assignment," she said.

I laughed out loud, then cringed as the sound reverberated. It was easy to imagine murderers in every aisle.

"You can put it on our transcript," I said. Hsing worked in the Department's office as part of her scholarship requirements.

"Let's get out of here."

We hurried downstairs, checked out the book, and ran back to our room.

"We're playing Sherlock Holmes," I said, opening the detective book with a flourish. "Okay, here we go."

I sat on my bed, and Hsing settled cross-legged on the floor. It was a warm evening even though the library hadn't been. From the open window, I could hear voices and laughter in the courtyard. They weren't worried about murderers.

I looked at the table of contents and turned to a chapter. "According to this, we have to find out three things. Number one is motive." Hsing's forehead wrinkled as though puzzled.

"Who would want to kill her?" I asked.

Hsing looked at me. Some expressions don't need translation.

"For example, Tomas," I said.

The one person in our class Miss Parker had conferred favored status on was Tomas Mann. He was a charming, older man whose mother was from Mexico and whose father was from Germany. Miss Parker favored him not because he was a cataloguer in the USC library (though only a junior one), but because she believed a rumor that he was a relative of the famous author who had relocated to Southern California. Tomas was not stupid, so he let her believe what she would. But I knew that he laughed at her fascination with famous people.

"If he doesn't get his degree," I said, "doesn't he have to go back to the clerical department? He wants to be a cataloguer in the Library of Congress." He had made no secret about his desires. In fact, almost everyone in library school wanted to work there: the epitome of the profession.

"More motive." She narrowed her eyes in concentration. "Scholarships."

"Good thinking," I said, trying not to look into those dark eyes, knowing how important her own scholarship was. Graduating meant that she could go back to her husband and baby daughter in China and work in the National Library at a well-paying job. Or any library, for that matter, as the Library of Congress system was used internationally. A degree for Hsing would also bring her prestige and respect. If she failed this class, she lost her scholarship, her student visa would be pulled, and she would be on the next flight home—to a not-so-nice drudge job. A thought snaked into my mind. Tomas's motive could also be Hsing's. I forced the snake to slither back out.

"Next?" Hsing said.

I jumped guiltily and looked back down at the page. "Second thing is opportunity."

Hsing frowned again. "Opportunity. Like fortune?"

I paged to the description. "Like being in the right place at the right time."

Hsing nodded. "Friday night people," she said as she leaned forward. "Next?"

"The third thing is means."

"Personage extinguish Miss Parker?"

I read through the paragraph. "The means—how the person was killed. In this case, the sword was on her desk, so he or she used it."

"I never do that," Hsing said, straightening her back.

"But if you were desperate enough," I said. "If your baby was hungry, you would kill. Wouldn't you?"

"No." She shook her head violently, her black hair flying. Then she ran out of our room.

I felt like biting my tongue. Too late, now, Kris. I knew how hard it was for Hsing to be away from her baby. How could I say such a thing? What was I thinking? Playing devil's advocate, but how to explain that?

I went down to the bathrooms and found Hsing standing in front of a sink, crying. I put my arms around her.

"I'm sorry."

"Ah, Kris, not what you say," she said, then after a moment she stepped back and looked at me. "I miss Sing Loo with all my heart. I do not want to think she is hungry. Never."

She pulled out a paper towel and wiped her eyes. I felt terrible.

"But you ask a clever question," Hsing said, her eyes still shiny with tears. "If Sing Loo hungry, and I have no food . . . maybe." Her face cleared of sadness, and I saw she was back on the hunt with me.

"So if I am with the will . . ." she made a plunging motion with her hands gripped around the pearl handle of the civil war sword.

For a moment I felt dizzy as I imagined the scene. I grabbed the edge of the sink and tried to refocus. Hsing, of course, had nothing in her hands but a crumpled paper towel.

"You mean who else would do what you would do?"

She nodded. We looked at each other in a way that translated to "a lot of people."

"How can we find out?" I said.

Hsing smiled. "Palace gossip."

"So let's go to it." I headed for the door.

"Here."

"What?" I looked around the ladies' room of the dorm. "Oh," I nodded, then shrugged.

Palace gossip. What the heck.

Just then the door swung open. I started washing my hands. Hsing fluffed her hair. Marcy, the perfect Palace gossiper and a Miss Parker Virginian, not that it had done her much good academically. I caught Hsing's look in the mirror. "You," was the message.

"Marcy, can you believe this?" I asked as breathlessly as I could manage. "Who would want to do in poor Miss Parker?"

That's all I had to say to get her started.

I saw Hsing's small smile in the mirror before she exited, off to find her own Palace gossip.

". . . and you know, she had a cousin heah." Marcy's voice rose on the last word just like Scarlett O'Hara.

"No," I said, but I seemed to remember something about that.

"She called him," Marcy drawled, "when she first got heah. And he hung up on her."

"He didn't," I said in the same Virginian accent.

"It's true. My second cousin knows his sister's boyfriend. And she said he told Miss Parker he didn't want anything to do with her *trashy* side of the family."

"No," I said in my best shocked tone. "But why would he want to kill her?"

Even Southern looks are translatable.

I wasn't too sure about the cousin. He could have killed her anywhere. However, since Miss Parker practically lived in her office, what better place?

Back in our room, Hsing and I went over what we had found out about who had motives.

"Too many," I said.

"Next item. Opportunity," she said.

I nodded.

"Friday night people."

It was my turn to be perplexed.

"Miss Parker went to her office after departure of class."

"That's right. I remember she told us all she was going to grade our term papers."

"Put sword in papers."

I could just see Miss Parker literally sticking that foot-long sword through our mid-term papers. They had been due at noon on Friday, no excuses accepted. No paper, no grade. No grade, no credit. No credit, no degree.

"All we have to find out is who was still here on Friday evening," I said, voicing the impossible.

"No problem," she said. "Just know work assignments. I know, I tell."

"Ohmygod, no! Hsing, don't say anything to anyone. We'll tell the police."

I had visions of both of us being stabbed in our beds, red blood on white sheets, with real swords sticking up out of the mess. I hadn't planned on ending my days while in library school.

"Kris, I tell *you*." Her dark hair swung around her ears. She made a sweeping, then mopping motion.

"Custodians," I said. "Of course."

"They come at six o'clock."

"Who are they?"

"List in office."

"The list of people who cleaned on Friday night is in the office?"

She vigorously shook her head and tapped herself on her chest. "Me," she said. "I am on the list."

"On the custodial list?" Of course. That was part of her scholarship duties, too.

"Come to office."

There, she pulled the list out of a file. "Work/Study," was at the top. The list was broken down with names under the headings of "Faculty," "Office," "Custodians."

She pointed to Bernie Cunningham and two other names. Not even real custodians. They worked as Hsing did, in exchange for classes.

I looked at all the other names. "What? Justin Rampart? But he's the assistant dean."

"Working on a Ph.D. in Library Administration. He and Miss Parker have noisy words Friday morning. Here."

"What about?"

"Miss Parker his advisor for Ph.D."

"Maybe she treated him like all her other students," I said. I hoped so.

Apparently someone had told the police about the "noisy words," because the next day they announced they were going to question Justin Rampart and everyone who had heard the exchange.

The cops—one short, one tall, in wash-and-wear suits with Goodwill ties—escorted Justin Rampart into Miss Parker's office. He looked white, as though he knew he was going to have a major operation without anaesthesia.

Hsing pulled me into the office next door, all the better to hear, because the office partition did not go all the way to the ceiling. I envisioned them taking him behind the desk where Miss Parker's dead form had sprawled.

"Whoever killed her must have been filled with hatred," one of them said, "because the murderer had to drive that sword in with a lot of force. She thrashed around before she died."

I shuddered at the thought.

"See this mark on the desk? That's where the sword hit after it went through her body."

A sound like a frog's croak came from the next room.

"Speak up, can't hear you Justin."

"I . . . I . . . see it." His voice sounded like his whole body was shaking.

"Now, I want you to look at this piece of paper." It was a different voice, had to be the other cop. "Preliminary forensic examination indicates that these two strokes of the pen were made *over* the blood."

Justin gagged.

"Do you know what that evidence tells us?"

Justin choked out a "no."

"It means the victim wrote it *after* she was stabbed."

"Ahhh . . ."

I was almost feeling sorry for Justin, but not quite.

"Read it, and tell us if it means anything to you."

Dead silence. Then a gasp and a moan. "C-C-C—," he stuttered then finally said the words as though they had been catapulted out of him.

"c973."

Hsing and I looked at each other. Her hands were over her opened mouth and her eyes were wide.

I grabbed her and pulled her down the hall into the lab.

We grabbed the elongated book that held the Cutter-Sanborn Tables.

We were both fumbling with it, trying to turn the pages.

We got to 'C', and ran our eyes down the columns to the end of the 900s.

There it was. We gasped.

The door opened.

Bernie Cunningham entered.

c973.

Cunningham.

The murderer.

We froze.

He looked from Hsing to me and then to the Cutter-Sanborn Tables.

I clutched the book to my chest like armor.

He knew we knew. We knew he knew. He came toward us. My heart stopped. Then he ran through the room and out the door on the other side.

A moment later the suits burst into the room with Justin in tow.

"Cunningham. Bernie Cunningham. He went that way." Hsing and I were talking and pointing at the same time.

For a moment the suits looked at us as though we were rehearsing lines in a play.

"c973," Hsing said.

They blinked in unison then dashed out the door after him.

Justin ran the other way.

It took me a minute before I could breathe again.

"He needed A for scholarship," Hsing said. She was panting too.

"An A! From Miss Parker?" I said. "You're right, he smokes his foot coverings."

She hugged herself as though she were cold and collapsed onto a chair. Suddenly, I felt my knees getting shaky, and I sat down, too.

"His term paper on the Cutter-Sanborn Tables," Hsing said.

I looked at her, realizing what must have happened. "Friday night, he was cleaning her office. She Cuttered his name while he was there, like she does in class. He should have known what the letter and numbers meant. If only he had taken that piece of paper, no one would ever have known. But why did he kill her?"

"Paper past time."

"But he had appendicitis. He should still be in the hospital. Surely . . ."

Hsing shook her head.

"You mean Miss Parker wouldn't accept his excuse?"

"Death only excuse," she said.

Dr. Gay Toltl Kinman *has published the preface to* The Catalog of the Los Angeles Police Department Library *and has written more* than 100 articles in writing, law enforcement, political, professional, and service organization publications, as well as many press releases in newspapers. She also co-edited Desserticide II for Sisters in Crime/Los Angeles. Her ten-minute play, "The Wicked Well," was produced in Cambria, California, and "Nicholas Owen," was stage-read at South Coast Repertory. She worked as a copywriter for a radio station and for ten years in the Los Angeles Police Department. She has a library degree and a law degree.

DRIVEN TO KILL

Jamie Wallace

I can't remember when I first decided to kill him. Once I made the decision, it wasn't hard to figure out how.

A loosened bolt, a weakened hinge, a sharp turn, and out he went, hitting the pavement hard. He rolled, tumbled, then with a sickening crunch landed beneath the wheels of the following car. I stopped as soon as I could. The shock of my action left me shivering and coughing on the side of the road. That's where they found me. The broken driver's side door and the skid marks told the tale.

Now I wait to learn my fate, anxious, but certain in the knowledge that he got what he deserved.

Maybe I should start at the beginning. My story began in the industrial heart of England. The year, 1958, started out gloomy and stayed that way. It was said that there were blue-sky sightings in the newspaper. I believe it. My earliest memories were of joint-stiffening cold, incessant rain, and gray skies, of tall, belching smokestacks and grime-ridden row houses.

Soon, I was sent to live with others of my kind. We lived in a big place with acres of concrete—no trees, no grass, no flowers, just glass and institutional brick walls.

Every day a parade of people would come in to look us all over. I'd stand proud, trying to look friendly and pleasant, to pretend that I was just like everyone else. But it was always the same: their enthusiasm disappeared when they took a closer look. They'd mutter what a huge commitment I'd be, then, using the feeble excuse that I was left-handed, they'd walk away eagerly to one of the others.

Over and over I'd hear them: "Left-handed? Who'd want one that was left-handed?"

There was nothing I could do. I came this way. A different arrangement of features. One by one my right-handed brethren went out the doors, through the gate and down the road. Loving families with excited eyes cooed sweet words before taking the others away to a new life.

I sat alone on the far side of the yard, watching with envy, longing.

Then one blessed day everything changed.

One of the staff told me they'd finally found someone who wanted me. He lived far away on the West Coast of America. Joy, excitement, and palpable relief flowed through me as they packed my trunk and shipped me off.

In the brilliant California sunshine I first glimpsed the kindly features of my guardian, my benefactor. The moment George Roberts saw me, his eyes filled with tears. I hesitated to go to him and stalled, but he came toward me, arms wide, an expression of pure love shining on his face.

"Oh, what a beauty you are. I've been searching for you for so long." He caressed me, his hands reassuring, gentle. "Come on now, it's time to go to your new home."

With a little coaxing, I finally ventured onto California soil. The warm, encompassing sunshine blinded me. I stalled again, afraid for a moment, but George murmured about the grand adventures in store, about how much he cared for me, how I would live with him always. Gaining strength from him, I made my way boldly into this new world.

The days, the months, the years that followed filled me with love and joy. I had my own comfortable room with everything I could ever want. True to his word, he never let me go hungry. We went everywhere together. I got to know his friends and soon became used to their admiring glances and open envy. Since I was the progeny of simple farming stock, I'd never thought of myself as beautiful, but under George's kind tutelage, I began to see myself as he did. I was proud and happy to be his family.

We lived in the desert where the sun shone almost every day. Gone were the bone-chilling rain and sleet of my early years. Even in the depths of winter, when the stars twinkled overhead in the brittle sky, I never felt the cold.

George adored the desert and the mountains, and he lived to drive. I learned to love it, too. I'd never experienced such exhilaration, such freedom as when we were out exploring the roads together. We'd spend hours, days, over the next twenty years climbing the ridges, speeding down twisting roads, top down, basking in the sun, the wind streaming past us. We left all of our cares and concerns in the dust behind. My deep affection for him grew with each passing moment.

Everything was as perfect as it could possibly be until the day that changed me forever. We were driving, George behind the wheel, exhilaration sparkling in his eyes. Suddenly, he grimaced and clutched his chest. Fear radiated from his every pore.

I tried to stop, to steer to the side of the road, but his other hand rigidly clasped the steering wheel. I saw the mountainside rushing toward us. When we hit the mound of dirt, I didn't care what happened to me. George was dead. The screeching sound of tearing metal rended my soul. I wanted to go with him.

They found me hours later, propped up on a pile of dirt, crying dark tears into the dust.

The next weeks, months, I spent alone, broken, battered. I felt my life's blood slipping away from me drop by drop. His adult children yelled, argued, bickered. They shouted so loudly I could hear every word—not that they cared. They blamed me for his death. Claimed I'd soaked up all his money and his time, argued that he'd loved me more than he'd ever loved them.

Eventually they turned me out. A kind friend of George's took me in, but the heart had gone out of me. After that I drifted from place to place, neglected and alone. I slept under tarps and scratchy blankets, and at other times lay exposed to the elements. My injuries healed, but the scars remained deep within me.

That's when I met him. He looked at me the same way George had. I tried to show him that I still had some spark left. He took me to his home that very day. Hope began to kindle again.

He consulted the best experts in their fields. They patched me up, dressed me up, smoothed my skin, made me whole again. Once more I began to look and feel like myself. I felt renewed, strong, beautiful.

Recovery took a long time, and he liked to take pictures to show my progress. I didn't mind. I gained confidence, began to breathe easier, had more energy than I'd had in years. Could one be so lucky to find two Georges in a lifetime?

I had my own room, a space really, filled with everything I could ever want, but it was sterile and lacked personality. I was grateful and didn't complain. Everything he did was done to immaculate perfection. No dirt dared fall, no dust bunnies dared linger, no liquid spilled without being wiped up.

I dreamed of George and our days exploring the deserts, the sun banishing the shadows from the sides of the arroyos. Of our exhilarating forays into the mountains, clinging to the roads through sheer force of will. Of screaming around turns, playing with momentum and inertia. I'd felt truly alive then. George always would occupy the deepest recesses of my heart, but it was time to open my soul to a new relationship.

This was not to be. The more time we spent together, the more I realized that he never really enjoyed my company, never actually cared about me. All he cared about was impressing his friends. I was merely a possession, a belonging. He didn't love me, only what I represented.

Worse than that, his obsessions grew. He became livid with any imperfection, was intolerant of the smallest speck of dirt, and screamed blue murder whenever anyone else touched me. He chose what colors and accessories I would wear. In short, he wouldn't put up with anything less than his version of perfection. I was simply a trophy.

My resentment grew, so I began planning. I stressed the door hinge on the driver's side; I loosened a bolt in the steering. He was too vain to wear a seat belt; it might crush his fine clothes. I bided my time and waited.

One day, my chance came. He was showing off during a road rally, racing well beyond the bounds of caution. I protested, but went along. A sharp turn, and nature took its course. The door flew open, the wheel spun, and out he fell, crashing, mangled beneath the wheels of the following car. Free, but fearful of the future, I was terrified of what lay ahead.

Now I wait for a new benefactor. I try my best to look strong and beautiful on the showroom floor. Will they notice the oil dripping from my crankcase? Will they care?

The sign near me says—1958 TR3 Triumph, recently rebuilt, drives like new.

I wait and hope that another George will come through the door.

Jamie Wallace is a recovering attorney who gave up the law for a life of crime writing. Former vice-president of Sisters in Crime/Los Angeles and active member of Mystery Writers of America, she is hard at work on two mystery series. A Los Angeles native, she has two men in her life, her adorable husband Bob and her equally adorable son Sidney. She can be reached via email at MsJames648@yahoo.com.

TOUCH OF A VANISH'D HAND

Phil Mann

The lecture concluded, mathematician Horace Masters thanked his audience and turned to erase the blackboard. Chalk dust sprinkled down and landed on the vest that covered his colossal chest and stomach.

"Professor Masters?"

A timid voice behind the large man caused him to turn. "Yes?"

The voice was that of a man in his twenties. He was frail, with blond hair and wire-rimmed glasses, which he pushed up on his nose. "I'm not quite sure how to phrase this," he stammered. "My name is Tony Reed."

The young man looked at Masters as if waiting for realization to dawn. The mathematician simply stared back blankly.

"I have a problem that might be well suited to your expertise," Tony said.

"My office hours are posted," Masters responded tersely. He turned back to the task of erasing the board.

"I was referring to a different sort of expertise. I've heard that you have some experience with locked rooms."

Masters froze, his hand perched high on the board. Tony did not know whether he expected Masters to turn around, his face aglow with the thrill of the challenge, or to respond in anger for Tony's brazen violation of the sanctity of the mathematical lecture hall. Masters did neither of these things.

Instead, he merely said, "I see," softly to the blackboard and continued erasing. "This wouldn't, by any chance, be for some screenplay, the sort of thing I'm told every other person in this town is trying to push?"

The young man laughed loudly, and *that* got Masters's attention.

Inside Masters's office fifteen minutes later, Tony searched for a place to sit. Masters had come to Pasadena as a visiting lecturer at CalTech only eighteen days earlier, and already he had amassed the sort of clutter some academicians spent entire careers trying to affect. Masters, however, seemed to have a natural flair for the disorganized welter of papers that Tony now saw.

"Have a seat," Masters offered, though there was no seat not already covered with papers.

"I'm comfortable, thank you," Tony said because he could think of nothing else to do.

"Why don't you tell me the story?" Masters asked. He collapsed into his large, leather chair and interlocked his fingers behind his bald pate. Unruly tufts of white hair jutted out at improbable angles.

"About ten days ago, Conrad Armstrong set up camp at my father's house. My father is a filmmaker, and Armstrong is—or was—an agent."

"Filmmaker?" Masters perked up. "I wonder whether I've seen his work. My wife and I just loved *The Sweet Hereafter*. Was that one of his?"

Tony smiled. "No, I doubt you've seen any of his stuff. All his movies are direct-to-video things. He calls them 'mature.' Video stores call them 'adult.' I think they're more accurately called 'soft porn.' They're also among the country's greatest cinematic representations of L.A. silicon that you're likely to find outside a Beverly Hills plastic surgeon's office. But that's neither here nor there. The thing is, this Armstrong was murdered about six days ago, and he had the gall to let it happen in my father's house."

Tony's voice lacked even a *soupçon* of compassion, and Masters sat slightly forward in his chair. "A bit harsh on the victim, aren't you?"

"Maybe," Tony conceded, "but Armstrong was the sort of guy you couldn't help but hate. There are all sorts of agent jokes, basically lawyer jokes with one word changed. But this guy was worse than all the punch lines. You've heard of the casting couch? He not only had one of those but also a turnstile. There were even tales that might have made de Sade proud. I don't know about those for certain, but I believe them. Everything he did seemed to be calculated to degrade someone."

"But your father invited him into your home?"

"He wanted Tawny Upton in his next film, and Armstrong represented her. But that's when the trouble really began. My half-brother, Vic, has a new girlfriend. She's an aspiring actress herself, and Vic used his obvious ties to get her a part in the movie."

"Your brother got his girlfriend a part in a blue movie?" Masters asked incredulously. "I have got to get back to the East Coast. There, men buy women dinner as part of the courting process."

"Maybe I oversold the films a bit. They're filled with large-breasted women running around with large guns. They're not actually the sort of thing they make in the Valley. Anyway, Tawny

Upton was Miss March last year, and she's very big in these films. But she didn't take to my brother's girlfriend. Her name's Rita, by the way. So Armstrong decided that he was going to demand that Rita's part be cut out of the film. He couldn't just insist on another actress. That would have been bad enough, but he had to demand that the entire part be removed. So he was spending a few days at dad's house rewriting the script."

"Wouldn't it have been easier for him to do it at his own home?"

"Maybe, but he was having it fumigated. Of course, his absence meant that the biggest rat would escape the toxic fumes."

Masters smiled. He liked the young man before him and had great difficulty understanding how such an intelligent fellow could come from the background he had described.

"Six days ago," Tony continued, "we found Armstrong dead inside the office he was using."

Masters pushed forward to listen intently. "Please," he urged, "do not omit any detail."

"I'll try not to. It was Saturday, and Armstrong had locked himself in the office in order to finish his changes. The office itself is a small room that opens into a hallway on one end and out onto the lawn by the cliff on the other end. It's a narrow room with bookshelves on the side walls. Well, they're shelves anyway. In theory, they could hold books, but it is my dad's house, so the theory remains untested. Anyway, nothing on the shelves seemed to have been disturbed.

"We found him at about four in the afternoon, but he'd been dead for a while already. You don't have to rely on my word for that. The police confirmed it. Rita was the one who found him. She was walking by and happened to look into the room, when she—"

"But I thought you said the room was locked," Masters interrupted.

"It was." Tony was momentarily puzzled, but he soon understood the source of Masters's confusion. "Oh, I'm sorry. You haven't seen the hallway door. The top half of it is a glass window. There's some glazed artwork that makes it translucent, but there is a border you can look through where there's clear glass. For whatever reason, Rita looked through, and she saw him covered with blood. She alerted everyone else, and we all gathered outside the door."

"And who is 'we' exactly?"

"That would be the five of us—myself, dad, Vic, Rita, and Linda. Linda's my father's new wife. She's his third. Or maybe his fourth. My mother was at least his second, and he's a little bit vague about his past before my mother."

"So the five of you were there. Did you unlock the door?"

"No. We couldn't, you see. The door's never really worked. A few years ago, someone broke the key off in the lock. We've never had the lock fixed. It still works from the inside. All you have to do is turn the lock. But you can't unlock it from the outside."

"Then how did you get in?"

"Vic told us to stand back, and he was about to break the window. But dad's wife nearly had a fit. The design on the window was done by an 'artist' she cultivated. That's her hobby. She goes 'slumming,' as she calls it, to find young artists she thinks have talent, and then she loses interest, and they return to wherever they came from. Anyway, one of them had done some work on one of dad's films and did an etching on the door. So Linda told Vic not to break the window but to go around to the outside instead. He did that, and the rest of us looked through the window.

"Vic tried opening the doors on the other end of the room. They're French doors. But Armstrong had chained them, so the doors only opened about an inch. Then Vic broke one of the windows and reached through to unlock the chain. He stopped at the desk for an instant to check Armstrong and then let us in."

"I see," Masters said enigmatically. "And you say that he was dead for quite some time before being discovered?"

"Yes. It's a good thing for Vic, too, because he'd be the obvious suspect otherwise. But . . . while I can't say that Vic's not capable of killing someone if provoked, I'm almost certain he had nothing to do with this. I almost could figure out how he could have pulled this off except for a few facts, and they make all the difference."

"Yes," Masters agreed, "it would have been a relatively easy trick to enter the room, kill the man, and then let the rest of you in."

"In some cases, perhaps, but not this one. Aside from the police statement that he'd been dead for hours, there's also the fact that his throat had been slit from ear to ear. There's no way that Vic could have done that with the four of us watching. And the room was locked. I both saw and heard Vic break the glass when he entered the room. And when he tried to open the doors beforehand, it was obvious that the chain was on. There's no way anyone could have faked that. So I'm stumped, and so are the police. I'd heard rumors about some of your exploits in the past, and I didn't know where else to turn."

"What about motives? Is there any way to narrow the question there?"

"I'm afraid not. I don't know too much about everyone else's dealings with the man, but I'm sure they all hated him. Other than what I've already told you, the only thing I can think of is that my dad's wife seemed especially hostile toward Armstrong over the past few days. And Rita's been rather depressed lately, but I suppose that's because Armstrong had threatened to remove her part from the film. My father—well, I didn't notice anything different about him. And Vic seemed his normal self. He never liked Armstrong and hadn't been shy about it. He never said anything directly to Armstrong, though, out of deference to my father."

Masters rose suddenly for no apparent reason that Tony could figure out. "I have work to do," Masters announced. "Be so kind as to leave me your address and phone number, and I shall call upon you tomorrow. Will four suit you?"

"Of course. Whenever you can. We're all very much in your debt for this."

"*All* of you?" Masters smiled mischievously. "That I tend to doubt. Let us make it at four, then. And please see that all the interested parties are present."

"A drawing-room revelation?"

"Of necessity, I'm afraid. I do not know who committed this deed. Oh! that reminds me. Everyone in your family was home that day and had an opportunity to kill him?"

"Yes, we were all there that day the whole day."

"Then you have presented me with a considerable conundrum. While I cannot be certain that I shall know by tomorrow, it is our only hope. I leave for the saner shores of the Atlantic on Sunday, and we are thus left only with tomorrow. If I am to be of any help, it will be tomorrow. Until then!" He rushed out of the room, leaving a relieved but perplexed Tony behind.

Masters felt obliged to attend the farewell dinner with some of the staff and students whom he had come to know during his visit to California. During dinner, however, his thoughts were on the room as Tony had described it. The rotund mathematician turned the problem over again and again, but there was one very important piece missing. He had called the detective investigating the case and been supplied with a few morsels of information, but the picture was far from clear. The missing piece did not manifest itself despite intense rumination during the remainder of the night or throughout the early hours of Saturday. Disappointed but determined to keep his appointment, he arrived at the Reed household in the Malibu hills at the appointed hour. Tony greeted him on the gravel driveway and agreed to Masters's request that he ask his stepmother to show Masters the room.

"I really don't know what you can expect to find," Linda Reed said as she led Masters down the hallway toward *the room*, as she had almost reverently referred to it. "The police pretty well cleaned it out."

They reached the room, and Masters made it his first point of business to inspect the etching on the window. He bent over awkwardly and stared intently. "This is remarkable," he said.

"Isn't it?" Linda asked rhetorically. It's an etching done by Julio Cortez. You've heard of him, of course."

He rose and looked at her blankly.

"The famous artist," she said, but the cloud remained on his face. "Surely you've heard of his work. Simply everyone has. Of course, when he did this, nobody had heard of him. I just recognized talent, and the boy was working on one of my husband's films, so he had to stay somewhere. Well, to make a long story short, he did this door to repay us since he couldn't afford anything else."

Masters, apparently no better educated than he had been before her attempt at edification, returned his gaze to the artwork. "Have you ever seen so pneumatic a woman in real life?" he asked in a deadpan voice. When she did not respond, he chose to rephrase his question. "She is rather, well, large, is she not? Surely, these are proportions Rostand could not have imagined—and in duplicate!"

"Is this Rostand person another artist?" she asked.

"Of a sort," Masters said. He returned his attention to the door. "So you can only see through the window at the edges. Interesting."

"Yes, that's glazing or frosting or some such thing," Linda added superfluously.

They entered the room, and Masters found it as Tony had described it. A moment was all he needed to convince himself that the hall door was without a secret. He experimented with the French doors and chain but could not find a way to disprove the story he had heard the previous day. There did not seem to be any way to lock the door from outside. "You're sure the door was locked?" he asked Linda.

"I saw the chain myself when Tony tried to open it. Both doors were locked."

"How can you be certain about the hall door?"

"We tried it. Before Vic tried to destroy that masterpiece, we both tried the door. Martin tried it, too."

"Martin?"

"My husband."

"Ah," Masters sighed. He opened the French doors and looked out over the cliffs to the Pacific Ocean below, a velvet expanse of blue maculated only by a few whitecaps and a lesser number of small boats. "It's an amazing view," he said. "Why does the desk face away from it?"

"Martin always felt the view distracted him."

"Harumph!" Masters snorted quietly. "Yes, I can see how natural beauty might disturb the process of creating showcases for the synthetic."

Linda seemed puzzled, but she shrugged off whatever had eluded her and smiled affectedly.

"And the chair there," Masters asked, indicating a leather arm-chair between the desk and the hall doorway, "is the only other furnishing?"

"Yes."

"So there's no place for someone to hide. Unless—" He pulled out the desk chair and peered beneath the desk. "No, this will not do."

Presently, he turned his attentions back to the French doors, inspecting them minutely. Only a single pane was absent from the doors. The missing glass was at about waist level, precisely where a person seeking to unlock the chain would have broken it. Masters noted curiously that the glass appeared to have been entirely removed. Around the edge of the empty space, a small gully formed by paint and putty belied the missing glass. Finding nothing more of interest, he stepped outside and looked at the ground, a hard, clay surface marked by a jumble of unreadable footprints. To either side of the clay was the meticulously main-tained lawn. Masters bent down and saw a small line of grass that appeared to have been matted down about three inches from the wall of the house. The line was about eight inches long, but its width could not be determined due to the imprecise surface. At best, the object had been half an inch wide, though Masters estimated a considerably smaller size.

He returned to the room. "I have seen enough," he said. From his tone, it was clear that he was not entirely pleased.

They left the room, but Masters turned the wrong way outside the door. He spied a line of photographs on the wall and immedi-ately realized his error. The other length of hallway had been bare. He leaned in close to the photographs to see them through the glare of the hall lights off the glass covering the pictures. Each frame seemed to hold a picture of Martin Reed on the set of one of his films. In many of the photographs, he was adorned by a bevy of scantily clad women. Masters sidled down the hallway until he came to a bare spot about a foot square.

"What was here?" he asked.

"You know, that's the strangest thing. It was a picture of me, but it disappeared mysteriously about a week ago."

Masters was suddenly at full alert. "When precisely?"

"Let me think. Yes, it was two days before Mr. Armstrong was—before we found him."

"Are you absolutely certain?" he asked excitedly.

"Yes, I am. The really strange thing is that we never found it. I'm pretty sure that Mr. Armstrong must have taken it, but I can't imagine why. Certainly nobody else would want a picture of me. And even if they did, they'd just have asked."

In the distance, a bell sounded a five-tone chime.

Linda looked up and said, "That's the doorbell. I wonder who that could be."

Rita McCarthy would have looked several years younger than her twenty-five years were it not for the excessive amount of makeup she was wearing. Masters suppressed a smile as he recalled an apt joke about putty knives.

"Linda said you wanted to talk to me?" She tucked a lock of blond hair behind an ear as if to help her hear his response. Her face was fixed in what seemed to be a subtle, morose pout.

"I was just wondering whether you might tell me something about Mr. Armstrong." He sat in the kitchen, an expanse of Formica and stainless steel, eating a sandwich that the Reed's servant had prepared.

"I don't know what you mean," she protested.

"Did you notice anything different about him? Did you perhaps see or overhear something?"

"Nothing that I can think of. I really didn't see him that much."

"I see. You've been wearing more makeup lately, I'm told." Masters was bluffing, but he was sure that she could not read him. To read a bluff, one had to have some familiarity with the bluffer, he was certain.

"Well, I knew he was going to write me out of the movie, and I thought if I gave him a more mature look . . . I just thought that maybe a subtle approach might help."

Masters looked up to see her smile, and he misunderstood the reason for the smile, which was that he had a prominent dab of mayonnaise on the side of his mouth.

"I think you might be interested to know," he said, "that it apparently worked. According to the detective to whom I spoke, the computer they confiscated revealed that your part remained in the film."

"Was there anything else you wanted to know?" she asked.

"No, I think that will do it. Let me finish my sandwich, and I will join you all in the den."

She gave him directions to the den and left him to his repast. When he had finished, he found that her directions had been precise, and he came upon a nervous group of five family members and two police officers, one of them a detective.

"Detective Nichols?" Masters asked.

"And you must be Horace Masters." Nichols extended his hand, which Masters shook.

Masters looked about the room and identified the two family members whom he had yet to meet. Recumbent on a sofa was Vic

Reed, a twenty-nine-year-old man who bore no resemblance to his half-brother. Vic was large and muscular with a head of wavy brown hair. Martin Reed was not wearing multiple gold chains as Masters had half expected, but the top three buttons of his shirt were undone, exposing a tangled mass of salt-and-pepper chest hair.

Masters looked about for a chair and spotted only a wire-and-canvas contraption that looked like the sort of thing one found only in dormitory rooms circa 1975 but not in places where taste and comfort were valued. He stared intently at the contraption, which surrounded a bucket seat with four peaks, and seemed to be trying to gauge its propensity for stability. At last, he lowered his considerable mass into the chair only to find his knee in close proximity to his chin. He moved to adjust his position, and the chair toppled over, dumping him unceremoniously on his posterior and on the hard floor. Mustering as much dignity as he could, he rose and brushed off the front of his vest. "Damnable design," he said tersely.

Somewhere in the room, a snicker escaped, and Masters's head darted up to scan the group. He pushed out his chest proudly and began.

"You will, I trust, forgive any repetition, but I think it is important to outline the salient facts so that you will see the merit in my little theory. We have two complicating factors. On the one hand, we have a room locked, I am convinced, from the inside at both means of egress. On the other hand, we have a megalo-maniacal victim, someone who created enemies everywhere he went, someone who seemed to revel in destroying others if only to assure himself of his own power. It is, you will admit, a curious combination. One factor, the hermetically sealed room, seems to suggest that nobody committed this crime. The other factor leads to an entirely different conclusion.

"I want to call your attention to the following facts. First, a picture of Mrs. Reed disappeared shortly before Mr. Armstrong met his demise. Second, the room in which he died affords no hiding space, save under the desk. Anyone there would have been visible to Vic when he entered the room, but even failing that, such a person would have been covered with blood. Third, Miss McCarthy has begun to wear more makeup than she did in the past. Fourth, in the grass outside the French doors, there is a small crease as if an object had rested there. Fifth, the victim was dead for a few hours before the discovery.

"Let us begin with the motive, which you will find conspicuous by the degree to which someone has gone to hide it. We know that Mr. Armstrong has a reputation for sexual conquests and sadism. It is reasonable to infer that the two have overlapped. At my suggestion, Detective Nichols checked phone records for the week before the murder. Detective, what did you find?"

"There was, as you suspected, a phone call from this address. Two officers investigated, only to be told that the call was a part of an experiment to add authenticity to a scene in a film. A man and woman assured the officers that everything was okay. The officers reprimanded the couple but took no further action."

"That call," Masters resumed, "was made by Miss McCarthy, and it was no hoax. Mr. Armstrong, I am convinced, attacked her. The legal term would be attempted rape. She managed to call the police, but she paid for it with a nasty bruise. Since that time, she has covered the bruise with makeup."

"That's not what happened at all!" Rita protested. "And I did *not* kill him!"

Masters raised a hand to stem her objection. "Nobody is accusing you of anything. Whether I am right in my conjecture about what happened is not entirely relevant, though I submit it for a better understanding of subsequent events. Now, where was I? Oh, yes. In a household that is used to the film industry, an excess of makeup might not be noticed. But one cannot wear makeup twenty-four hours a day. So it was inevitable that *someone* would notice eventually. And someone did.

"I will now tell you what the killer did. He removed a picture of Mrs. Reed from the wall in preparation for an act he probably did not wish to commit. For two days, he sought evidence that would refute his suspicions, but none was forthcoming. Finally, he lost his patience. He was ready to act. Armstrong was locked inside the study, working furiously on the rewrite of the script. I am told, incidentally, that an agent rewriting a script is almost unheard of, but I am also told that most agents are generally ethical. Clearly, Armstrong was singular in more than one way.

"The killer went to the French doors, where nobody but the victim would see him. He entered the room, presumably without breaking the window. At that point, he confronted Armstrong and demanded to see the script. What he was looking for was whether Miss McCarthy's role was still in the film. As it turned out, Armstrong had reinstated the scene. That, ironically, was his fatal error. The killer now had the evidence he sought, and he murdered Conrad Armstrong."

"But why?" Linda Reed asked.

"Because he was convinced that his girlfriend was having an affair with Armstrong and that the role was the payback for that dalliance," Masters said with a verbal flourish.

Vic seemed suddenly to realize that he was the object of Masters's reference, and he shot to his feet prepared to protest. He had not noticed, however, that the uniformed officer had inched toward him. The officer put her hand on his shoulder, pushed him down, and read him the Miranda warning. Vic twice seemed about to protest his innocence, but he thought better of it and exercised his right to remain silent.

Masters, unfazed by these events, waited until attention was once again focused on him. "Victor Reed misread the evidence. He had seen the bruising on his girlfriend's face and was aware of Armstrong's penchant for violent sexual games, but Vic seemed unable to grasp the concept that his girlfriend might not have been a willing participant. The role in the film was, I am convinced, in exchange for her silence when the police responded to her call and not in contemplation of future meretricious services."

Vic looked at Rita with a question in his eyes. She nodded almost imperceptibly and then averted her gaze.

"After Vic killed Armstrong, he broke the window and removed all the glass, leaving an empty rectangle. He closed the doors and reached through to slide the chain in place. All he had to do then was dispose of the glass and the weapon and wait. Eventually, the alarm would come. And it did. He took a slight risk when he appeared ready to smash the glass of the window in the hall door, but this risk was not all that great. Mrs. Reed's fondness for that noisome adornment was well-known, and he could rely upon her to object. Even in the unlikely event that she did not object, he no doubt would have had a sudden epiphany and pointed out the sacrosanct nature of the door. But she did as he expected, and he went around to the French doors as he had planned.

"There, he picked up a piece of glass that he had previously leaned against the house. That glass, I expect you have figured out, came from the picture of his mother that he took two days previously. While he opened the door to demonstrate that the chain was indeed in place, he slid the glass into place over the empty spot in the door. He could rely on the four people in the hall not to notice. They would have been focused on the chain or the body. Once the piece of glass was in place, he broke it. That is why you both saw and heard glass break.

"The rest you know." His oration over, Masters seemed tired. He looked for a place to sit but found only the chair that had already demonstrated an antipathy for him. His sigh was lost amid a sea of voices that was rising to fill the room. The click of handcuffs sounded as Masters left the room.

On a 747 bound for Boston, Masters pulled his wallet from his inside jacket pocket and flipped the leather open to reveal a small photograph of his wife. Yes, the East Coast would be a welcome sight, he thought.

Phil Mann is an attorney living in Los Angeles.

AI WITNESS

Kate Thornton

The precision with which the blade sliced through the pink flesh, neatly separating it into six equally beautiful and symmetrical pieces, sent a chill down my spine. Or maybe it was the air-conditioning. They always kept it too cold in the Ai, but it was my favorite sushi bar.

The graying hostess in the baggy blue-and-white apron had shown me to the bar, one seat from the corner, with all the other high, backless chairs occupied by the usual weeknight crowd. I spotted a few strangers from nearly a dozen faces, and I got a friendly nod from the rest as I slid into a seat. This wasn't my usual night, but I'd had a hard day at work, and it wasn't over yet. The chef grinned across the flayed *maguro* and set a rectangular china plate in front of me.

I sipped my hot tea and waited patiently. The young chef would get to me sooner or later, and half the fun of the place was that it could take you all night to eat a couple of expensive pieces of raw fish. The little glass front refrigerator case that ran the length of the counter held only the freshest fish and shellfish, colorful and with interesting textures. But I knew all of it would be gone by closing time. The sushi had to be absolutely fresh, and even a few hours could make a difference.

I leaned back and listened in on the conversation of the ladies to my left as the chef sliced up a few freebie snacks for them.

The bar provided an illusion of companionship and camaraderie as well as dinner, and I settled in for an evening of pleasant dining and overheard conversation.

I waved and indicated that I would have an order of *maguro* sashimi, sliced tuna over threads of raw daikon. A beginner's dish, the raw tuna was easy to eat. It was also one of my favorites. Some of the dishes were more exotic and expensive because of the rarity of their ingredients, but I chose plain tuna.

"Kevin's just so demanding," one of the ladies to my left was saying. She looked about thirty, with wispy blonde hair and a little too much makeup over one eye. "You know, if he even thought I was out here tonight, he would be furious!"

"Well, what I don't know is why you stay with him," the other one replied. She was smaller, dark-haired and intense. "Face it, Irene, he treats you like dog meat, and you just put up with it. I would have left him years ago."

"Oh, Patty, I've looked at my choices. Divorce is just so expensive," Irene said in her defense. "I would be left penniless. I have no skills, no education, no job. Where would I go, what would I do?"

"Well, it's a good thing you don't have any children," Patty said angrily. Then her features softened. "Aw, I didn't mean to make you feel bad. Let's look on the bright side. At least he works late, and you can meet me here every Tuesday evening for dinner."

She held up her bottle of Kirin, and Irene clinked her own against it. "And we have this to look forward to!"

"But it's true. If he even thought I was out of the house, he would never let me forget it," Irene said. "And the very idea of sushi turns his stomach. Why, he would no sooner eat raw fish than he would chew gum from the bottom of a movie theater seat!"

They both dissolved into giggles at the thought of this. "But he sure does like other kinds of food," Patty noted. "I've seen him eat three large pizzas with everything on them—and I mean everything—and not even burp."

"You're lucky, then," Irene replied. "I get to see him burp, too!" They started laughing again. Then, so quickly and unobtrusively that I would have missed it if I hadn't looked up just then to flag down the busboy and get a beer, Irene slipped something into her purse.

I bent over my plate of *hamachi* sashimi. Sometimes the things I heard were private, and I tuned them out. But other times, I listened eagerly. I felt like I knew these women—at least Irene of the swollen face and demanding husband. I had seen other women like her, women whose husbands kept them locked up and disciplined. I wanted to learn more about her, so I cocked an ear toward them, but I didn't make eye contact. I wanted to hear more about their lives, and I knew that if I made conversation, it would just be the polite exchange of acquaintances at a sushi bar. Like I said, the feeling of intimacy and camaraderie was mostly an illusion. We didn't know each other, not really.

The two women talked more about Patty's job at the insurance office, and Irene said wistfully that she wished she could have a job or something. "But," she laughed, "Kevin says he's my job, my one and only full-time job." She laughed again, then frowned. "And it's true. He is a full-time job. One I wish I could quit."

I shifted on my high barstool a bit and waved to the chef for another order. I watched out of the corner of my eye to see if

Irene put anything else in her purse.

My order of *unagi*—broiled eel brushed with a sweet teriyaki sauce—arrived, and I delicately picked up one of the two pieces with my chopsticks. It was my idea of dessert, sweet and savory and—unlike most things at the sushi bar—cooked. But I noticed that Patty and Irene had the big sampler tray of delicacies like thinly sliced raw fish, rice-wrapped bits of raw squid, and things I didn't recognize. They were either fond of sushi or very adventurous, I thought. But there was something about Irene that looked beaten down and not very adventurous at all.

I saw a tiny movement out of the edge of my vision and watched as Irene put another piece of something into her purse. This made no sense to me. Nothing spoils faster—or would be more of a mess in someone's purse—than raw fish. Not even my cat, Bertie, would touch leftover sushi.

I watched and listened and toyed with my final cup of hot barley tea. Patty and Irene talked about fashions and sales and then about beauty treatments and magazines they had read. They laughed and giggled and looked more like schoolgirls than grown women. When Patty tipped the chef and got up to leave, I asked for my check, too. I watched Patty and Irene hug each other and go their separate ways: Patty to a big sedan in the back parking lot, and Irene to a waiting taxi.

I sighed and started walking. It was a beautiful evening, and my work was finished. I walked back to my office to type up my report, but I didn't mention anything about the sushi in Irene's purse.

Later that week, when I read the newspaper article buried on page ten of the daily edition, there was nothing to connect the Ai with the death of Kevin Foster. In fact, his death was blamed on a virulent infection from a couple of spoiled pizzas.

But I knew better. I knew better even as I watched Irene Foster put the pieces of fresh raw fish into her purse. I knew better the morning after my visit to the Ai when I handed Kevin Foster the private investigation report I had just done on his wife.

I don't always like my clients, especially when they are domineering wife-beaters, but I usually ignore it and give them what they pay for—in this case a report of Irene's Tuesday evening dates.

Kevin wasn't too happy with what I found out. He had been certain that she had been cheating on him, not just escaping out to dinner with a girlfriend once a week, even though the thought of Irene doing something without his permission enraged him. I guess the real turning point though, was when he accused me of lying to him and being involved with her. That did it. I handed him the report, took his check, and showed him out the door without another word.

But looking back, I guess I should have said at least one more word. I should have at least whispered a warning—one he could take to heart the next time he had a pizza.

I should have whispered, "*Anchovies.*"

Kate Thornton began writing short mystery and crime stories several years ago. She finds inspirations in the petty tyrannies of everyday life and spends a great deal of her time listening in on other people's conversations. She writes science fiction when not turning to crime and has an extensive online following in popular e-zines. Visit her website at www.sff.net/people/katethorton.

OVER MY SHOULDER

Lisa Seidman

That man is watching me again. He doesn't think I see him, but I do. Ever since we came to Florida he's been following me with his eyes, catching me through uncurtained windows, watching me through the screened back porch of my grandparents' apartment as I read my Gothic novel. His eyes are like the high beams of a car's headlights, trapping me in their bright, focused, unmoving glare.

I used to catch glimpses of him when I was ten or eleven; I'd see him out of the corner of my eye, then, when I'd turn around quickly to surprise him, he'd disappear.

But I knew what he looked like: a little over medium height, with stooped shoulders and fingers yellow with nicotine. He smelled of ashes and stale beer. I called him Mr. Brown. He even drove a brown Ford sedan, and I imagined him sitting in it all day outside my elementary school, waiting for me to separate from my friends, go down a deserted alley or cut through a dark and empty parking lot, so he could offer me a Hershey bar or a bag of M&M's and lure me into his car and disappear with me forever.

But in those days I was too smart for him. I walked the well-lighted streets of my Long Island town, always surrounded by friends, never once veering from the norm. I stopped looking for him out of the corner of my eye, hoping that if I ignored him long enough he'd eventually go away.

Even when Jimmy Panzarino, the class bully, threw a snowball made mostly of ice that hit me squarely in the back and hurt me all the way home, even then, I didn't look around. Everyone thought I was so brave: I didn't cry, I didn't retaliate. Jimmy never got any satisfaction from that ice ball he threw. But it had nothing to do with Jimmy. I just didn't want to see Mr. Brown sitting in his brown Ford, smoking his cigarettes and eating the M&M's I refused to take from him. I didn't want to see his sorrowful expression; I didn't want to hear him say, "Come sit with me. I'll remove the ice chips from under your collar. I'll rub your back. I'll make it all better."

Mr. Brown thought he wanted to take care of me, but I knew all he really wanted was for me to die.

When I turned thirteen, Mr. Brown followed me to junior high. I still wore an undershirt under my first bra. The girls in my gym class looked at me funny because of that undershirt, but no one said anything. In a moment of weakness I told my best friend Nancy Shilay about him. Nancy looked at me scornfully. "You always did have an overactive imagination," she said.

At that moment I realized that man was my problem and no one else's.

He trailed me to Florida with my family. I don't know how he did it; his brown Ford sedan didn't follow our air-conditioned Hertz rental through the open wrought-iron gates of my grandparents' retirement community. But as soon as I bounded outside my grandparents' apartment, after changing into shorts and T-shirt, there he was, no longer in the corner of my eye, but standing in full sight, walking around the corner of the apartment as if to greet me.

"Hey, Susie, look at you . . . you've got legs!"

His eyes moved up from my bare legs, still white from the New York winter, to my shorts, then raked my skimpy T-shirt. He gave me a wolf whistle.

"You're all grown up now. When did that happen?"

I stared at him in shock. He knew my name! Instinctively, I folded my arms against my chest, standing frozen, quivering in fright, until the screen door banged open, and Mom stepped outside. She seemed nervous, although I couldn't tell whether she saw the man or not.

"Susie, why don't you come inside and talk to Gran and Grandpa? They want to hear about school."

Obediently and with great relief, I walked past her and headed back inside the apartment. Mom never said a word about the man, but I noticed she closed the front door rather firmly when we were both back inside, not looking at me as she busied herself with emptying the ashtrays already filled with my father's cigarette butts.

The Florida trip was spoiled for me from then on. Everywhere I went, that man was lurking. I stopped wearing shorts and T-shirts and boiled in my jeans and baggy blouses instead. My sister Rachel and Grandpa made fun of me. Mom looked on silently, not telling them to keep quiet, but pursing her mouth in a thin, pained line every time they teased me. Did she see that man, too? If so, why didn't she say anything about it? I thought about asking her, but what if she acted like Nancy Shilay and told me I had an overactive imagination? If I was losing my mind, then I didn't want anyone else to know about it.

My father was on a mobile home kick that summer and insisted we check out the sales lots looking for the perfect mobile home to which he and Mom could retire. When I protested being dragged along, his eyes narrowed, and he mashed out a half-smoked cigarette. "No whining from you, young lady. You'll come because I say you will." When he stalked out the door, Mom put an arm around my shoulders.

"It's a phase he's going through," she said. "Just go along with it, and he'll get over this mobile home thing eventually."

But in front of Gran and Grandpa, my father was relaxed and cheerful. "I love Florida," he announced during the Early Bird dinner at Manero's one evening. Gran's mouth knit a thin line of disapproval as he drank from a stein of beer, wiping the foam from his mouth with a careless sweep of his hand. "Never mind retirement, maybe we should think about moving down here now."

Rachel clapped her hands in agreement, and Mom smiled. But I couldn't share their enthusiasm. I saw Mr. Brown at the pool, in the apartment; he even followed me to the mall. I longed to be alone but didn't want to be separated from my family. They could protect me. I volunteered to go grocery shopping with Mom and Gran, humored my little sister by seeing the latest Walt Disney revival at the local theater as often as she wanted. Took long walks with Grandpa. I was the best daughter, sister, and grand-daughter anyone could ask for, but he still wouldn't go away.

At night, lying on the fold-out couch in the den with my sister, sweating slightly, I would listen for the rustling of palm fronds outside the window.

Was he out there, trying to look in? Rachel demanded we leave the sliding glass doors open because my grandparents refused to run the air-conditioning at night. What would stop him from slipping inside, staring at me to his heart's content while I lay asleep, oblivious? I knew my sister couldn't protect me. She didn't even know the man existed.

Then, one day, I let my guard down. I was tired of my family, tired of lying awake at night in fear. "Please let me stay home and nap," I said when they told me they were off to the movies at the local mall. My father offered to stay and keep me company, but I said no. I just wanted to lock all the doors, turn up the air-conditioning full blast, crawl under the covers and sleep for hours.

They left me. I slept.

A noise jerked me awake. Eyes open, I stared at the closed bedroom door, body trembling. Were they back so soon? Why didn't I hear Mom and Grandma gossiping, or the rumble of Grandpa's voice? Why didn't my sister rush in and pounce on me? Why did I just hear one person, breathing heavily, on the other side of the door?

The door started to open.

I closed my eyes, pretending to be asleep. It was that man. He had gotten inside the apartment. Somehow.

"Susie."

It was him. Whispering. Voice slightly hoarse. I kept my eyes shut. I smelled his ashy smell and tried not to gag.

"Susie, it's me."

The voice was closer. I hoped he couldn't see me trembling under the knitted afghan. Gran tried to teach me how to knit that visit. But I was always looking out for that man and couldn't concentrate.

"Susie, wake up."

He was standing right next to the sofa bed. I could sense his shadow lying over me. I stayed frozen in place, my eyes glued shut.

He did nothing for a moment; I could tell he was just staring at me. I prayed he'd go back out the door; I prayed Mom would come home now.

But then he reached down, hands tugging at the afghan. I gripped the edge of the blanket and held on. Would he still believe I was asleep?

"It's just you and me, Susie. I'm not going to hurt you. I love you."

Abruptly I was caught off guard, and he ripped the blanket from my body. Without even thinking, I opened my eyes, stared at him . . . that man . . . Mr. Brown.

"I knew you were up. Won't you let me love you?"

His smile was gentle, but his eyes looked dirty and afraid. His hands reached down to caress my face, my neck.

"I've always loved you, you know. Ever since you were a little girl, I could sit and watch you for hours . . . you're so beautiful."

All those years of surrounding myself with friends, of walking well-lighted streets, all for nothing. He ignored my tears as they slid down my cheeks, onto his caressing hands. I tried to squirm away.

"No . . . don't. Please go away. I won't tell anyone . . ."

"But I love you so much," he said as his hands moved down past my neck, gently starting to unbutton my short-sleeved cotton blouse.

Afterwards, I was filled with energy. I don't know why I didn't have it to help me fight him off, but now I took a vigorous, scalding shower, washed the bloody, sticky sheets, changed my clothes, and walked to the dumpster to throw out the ones he removed from my body. I was afraid to go outside in case some- one saw me and figured out what happened. I was convinced I was wearing a sign around my neck, or that the neighbors could read it on my face. But I couldn't stand another minute having those clothes in the apartment, so I shoved them in a brown grocery bag, crumpled up the bag as tightly as possible, and strode to the dumpster, where I pushed them under a pile of old newspapers and white plastic trash bags. I didn't tell Mom what happened when everyone came back, laughing and chattering from the movies. They had lost my father for a while when he decided to see a different movie and was late meeting them at Morrison's Cafeteria in the mall for lunch. My sister giggled that they were ready to plaster his picture on milk cartons, but then Mom found him having a beer at the Steak 'n Brew at the other end of the mall and everything was all right.

The man continued to watch me, although I made sure I was never alone. But I couldn't eat, and I couldn't sleep. Mom grew worried.

"Is everything all right?" she asked one day at the mall as I looked dispiritedly at some cotton shirts. One of them was exactly like the one I had thrown out, and I started to shake.

"Honey, what is it? What's wrong?"

But how could I tell her? A man has been watching my every move for as long as I can remember, and he did terrible things to me while everyone was away. I often imagined telling her, but I could only picture her look of disbelief and denial. And that would be even more awful than what had already happened. So I only shook my head and smiled.

"Think I'm getting a cold."

We went straight home, and she fed me aspirin and hot tea. Colds she could handle.

He followed me home from Florida. I couldn't ask my sister to sleep in my room at night. I thought of asking for a lock on my bedroom door but didn't have the strength for explanations. So I kept silent even though Mr. Brown grew bolder. I knew if I screamed, no one would hear. If no one else saw him, how could he exist? But if he didn't exist, why did I dread the night, and why did it hurt between my legs so much afterward?

A few weeks after school started my little sister Rachel came to my room. I was pretending to do homework as she sidled up to me, looking over her shoulder as if afraid of being overheard.

"Susie, can I ask you something? And do you promise not to tell Mommy I asked you?"

I never had much time for my little sister, especially then, so I barely looked at her as I answered. "I promise not to tell. What is it?"

Rachel paused, seemed to gather her courage. "Do you know Mr. Brown?"

My head swiveled so fast I felt a tendon in my neck cramp. Rachel looked away, frightened. I realized: My little sister was ten years old, just about my age when that man started lurking outside my elementary school.

"How do you know Mr. Brown, Rachel?"

The words came out too sharp. Rachel took one last frightened look at me before bolting out of my room.

She wouldn't talk to me about Mr. Brown after that. But I could tell he started hanging outside her window at night like one of those corpses in *Night of the Living Dead*, which a bunch of us watched at Nancy Shilay's sleep-over party. He was probably loitering across the street from the elementary school again. Rachel kept glancing over her shoulder, as if trying to catch something in her peripheral vision. She jumped when anyone called to her and walked past the bowl of M&M's Mom kept in the living room without giving them a second look. I knew I had to do something before Mr. Brown got into Rachel's room like he was getting into mine.

One afternoon during band practice on the football field, my friend Laurie Goldstein confided in me that she had thought about committing suicide. When no one was home, she said, her nose stud glittering in the afternoon sun, she took the largest knife she could find from the middle kitchen drawer and brought it to her wrist.

"One sharp quick cut. That's all it would take." She bobbed her head in confirmation, tucking back a dyed pink strand behind her ear. "But I didn't have the guts. So I put the knife back in the drawer and walked away." She stared at the empty bleachers in front of us. "I wonder if it would've hurt much," she murmured. "I wonder if there would've been a lot of blood."

I stayed late after school the next afternoon and missed the bus. It was a long walk home, but I called my folks from a pay phone outside the school and assured them I'd be fine. I'd enjoy the exercise as well as some peaceful time alone to myself.

It was a crisp, fresh evening, the clouds thin and white against the October sky. But it was getting dark and cold, and as I passed a narrow, unlit alley I realized it would cut ten minutes from my time. I refused to look over my shoulder as I entered it but carefully slipped the kitchen knife from my backpack and waited for Mr. Brown to follow me inside.

I've never enjoyed spending Christmas in Florida, but ever since my grandparents moved down here, hot, sunny, snowless Christmases have been a fact of life for our family. This one, however, is particularly bad. Mom can't stop crying, and Rachel clings to her knees like a two-year-old, screaming if Mom so much as leaves the room without her. It's scary seeing Mom cry, even more so because she doesn't bother to hide it from Rachel and me. When she's not lying on one of the twin beds in my grandparents' darkened bedroom, she's slumped in Grandpa's easy chair, staring out the window, an unread mystery sitting in her lap. I know she's worried about Grandpa, lying with tubes up his nose in the hospital. I should be worried about him, too. But I've got other things on my mind.

Because, you see, that man is back. I thought I killed him in that trash-strewn alley on a side street in my hometown. But when the local paper reported his death, they gave him a different name, claiming he was probably murdered by another homeless man for whatever money or alcohol he had on him. I wanted to tell Laurie Goldstein that it does hurt—the man screamed and screamed. And there was a lot of blood. Not that it matters now. Obviously, I failed. Instead of being gone forever, he's back lurking around the corner, staring at me as I read, following my sister and me as we head for the pool.

So, once again, I've stopped wearing shorts and T-shirts. I no longer go swimming, feeling embarrassed and on display in my one-piece bathing suit. Even when Rachel cries hysterically, and Mom can't take it anymore and asks me to get her out of the house. Even when she snaps at me, "Susan Rae Brown, just once in your life will you please act your age and do what you're told?"

Even then, I refuse.

I'm lying on the back porch now, pretending to read my Gothic novel, trying to ignore that man's greedy look. Sulking, Gran calls it. I wish I could tell her the truth. But I know deep down she's really worried about Grandpa. Besides, I know she won't believe me. A shadow falls across my lap, and I look up. My father stands before me and I tense, thinking he is going to yell at me for my behavior. Instead, he smiles.

"Come on, Susie . . . Why don't you, Rachel, and I hit the beach?"

That means getting into a bathing suit, and I don't do that anymore. Which is what I tell him. But he still smiles, and I can tell he's in his "I'm not taking 'no' for an answer" mood.

"I don't care what you wear. Mom and Gran are going to the hospital to visit Grandpa. So why don't we get out of the house, too? Unless you want to go with them?"

My father knows that's the last thing I want to do. The smell of hospital disinfectant is almost worse than Mr. Brown's cigarette smell—or his stare. And I can't stand to watch Grandpa cry at his own pain and helplessness. Not because he's in pain, but because I'm jealous he can show it.

"Okay," I say. "Let's go to the beach."

My father is suddenly happy. "Great. I'll tell your sister, and we'll leave in ten minutes."

Ten minutes. Enough time to grab a knife from Gran's left-hand kitchen drawer and wrap it in a beach towel tucked under my arm. This time I will wear a bathing suit and lie in the sun and maybe get a little tan. I'll even smooth sun block slowly over my legs and thighs and let my arms swing at my sides instead of keeping them crossed at my chest. I'll stand up straight and stroll leisurely across the sand to the little-used showers and toilets at the far end of the beach. Because I know Mr. Brown will follow. Afterwards, I'll ask Mom to take me to the mall. Shorts and T-shirts are on sale at The Gap. I want to stock up for the summer.

Lisa Seidman *is a television writer who's written episodes for* Cagney & Lacey *and* Murder, She Wrote *and has been a story editor and executive story consultant on* Falcon Crest, Dallas, *and* Knots Landing. *She's been nominated for a Writers' Guild Award for her work on the Aaron Spelling daytime soap,* Sunset Beach.

THE CATS AND JAMMER

Gayle McGary

Jammer knew who the murderer was: "It's Mrs. Moore." He jumped off the couch and moved to the window. He pushed the blinds apart and peered out into the courtyard. It was not quite five a.m., and the early light was just skimming the red tiled roofs of the bungalow court, casting cool shadows. Sure, it has to be her, he thought; the weird old lady in bungalow number one. He could see the glint of the brass knocker in the shape of a cat's head on her door directly across the court.

Jammer moved back to the couch and picked up his script. He wrote:

```
        DETECTIVE JAMES 'THE JACKNIFE' LOGAN
You could never tell who might be a cold-blooded killer.
There's a dark place in each of us. Who can ever know
what small thing it might take to open its yawning maw.
```

Jammer crossed out "its yawning maw" and wrote "it." Satisfied, he leaned back and yawned himself. He'd been up all night.

Jammer had written half a dozen screenplays, all stinkers according to his brother, a successful writer and director himself. Convinced that school was a waste of time for a writer, Jammer dropped out as soon as he turned sixteen. His brother had had a shit fit and bribed him with an offer of the manager's job at this old Hollywood bungalow court he owned. The offer came with a little responsibility, not too much work, and lots of time to write, but only if he passed the high school equivalency test, the GED. It was an offer he couldn't refuse.

So far, all of his screenplays had been in the film noir genre. It wasn't bad writing, said his brother, but the plots were cliché-ridden rip-offs of Tarantino or Thompson or Towne. Jammer thought they were hot, but his brother said, "Write what you know." Jeez, thought Jammer, what do I know? I'm sixteen years old and live in this old dump of a court in Hollywood.

Jammer peeled a dab of mozzarella off the pizza box lid, raised it and lowered it into his mouth, head at a tilt, as he walked back to the window. He tweaked the blinds open again and thought about his fictional murderer. Mrs. Moore was perfect. She gave the appearance of being a harmless little old lady, but maybe she had a dark place. He'd have to make her younger and more attractive. In real life she was frowzy haired and dumpy in polyester pink sweatsuits. She scuffed around in ratty slippers with cutesy animal heads on the toes. Jammer thought she must have a regular zoo of bunnies, kitties, monkeys, puppies, and raccoons in her closet. A different animal every week. The other tenants called her the Cat Lady because she fed an army of stray cats that came down from the hills in the early morning hours.

Jammer could see the old lady's cats beginning to gather in the courtyard now. They perched here and there, in shafts of sunlight, among the shaggy banana palms, in singles and in bunches.

They licked and scratched and watched for the door of bungalow one to open and breakfast to be served. They would make a good visual touch to his script, add a little menace.

Jammer let the blinds slide shut. As manager, he should probably do something about the cats. He'd bet there was some law about the health hazard of having so many cats around. They began arriving before dawn, and territorial disputes broke out. There were yowling matches six nights out of seven. Last night had been lucky seven, unusually peaceful and quiet. Hey, live and let live. That was his Personal Rule Number One. Anyway, the other tenants didn't make much of a fuss except to throw shoes and beer cans when the squalling went on too long.

Jammer went back to the couch and put on his running shoes. Bright cartoon characters bashed each other on the screen of the long-muted TV. He'd been on a roll last night, writing straight through prime time, Nick at Nite, the early morning movies. He was wired and hungry. Maybe as hungry as those cats out there. He adjusted his headphones and headed for the door, picking up his skateboard in the hall. He'd go out for something to eat. He stuck his notebook in the pocket of his baggies. He still had to decide *how* and *why* the Cat Lady committed the murder.

Outside, Jammer glanced again at Mrs. Moore's bungalow with the well-kept rose garden in front. Near the gate and directly across from him, the intervening space between them was filled with cats. They didn't look menacing; they looked scruffy and pitiful. He would write the menace.

The tenants of his bungalow court were a colorful cast of characters. He could have made a case for any one of them committing murder. For instance, Monica Lexus, the aspiring actress in bungalow number four who worked the Hard Rock Café in more ways than one. She owned a red sports car but rarely drove it, always managing to get rides home after work. The men left hours later, sometimes staying long enough to give her a ride back to work. She could be a murderer.

Or Alphonse Fredericks in number two. By his own account he was a famous but now retired actor. To Jammer, he was your basic weirdo. Fredericks made a living selling by mail order such items as whips and chains, rhinestone bulldog clips for nipples, and spike-studded leather jock straps with the spikes on the inside.

On the other hand, Jammer found it easier to see these two as murder *victims*: Monica murdered by one of her pickups who turns out to be a serial killer, or Fredericks S&M'd to death by one of his customers.

Jammer hopped on his skateboard and began to circle the court, his head abuzz with the possibilities. He needed to focus on means and motive for Mrs. Moore being a murderer.

"Hellooo, James," Mr. and Mrs. Cleveland hailed him from bungalow three. They were walking toward the alley garages. "We're off to see the wizard. Ha, ha."

They wore plaid shorts, matching Disneyland T-shirts, and cameras slung about their necks. Jammer knew they were off to spend the day bagging shots of celebs on the Strip. As murder suspects for his screenplay, the Clevelands had run a close second to Mrs. Moore. Middle-aged retirees from the Midwest, the kind of people who complained about their arthritis and paralyzed you with stories about their grandchildren, they seemed so unlikely as cold-blooded killers. There were, of course, the mysterious meetings they held Wednesday nights with an ever-changing lineup of men. He could make something of that.

Jammer rolled past Louis St. Grandam's bungalow. It was too early for the insurance claims adjuster to be out in the BMW he kept parked in front of the court and where he spent most days on his cell phone. That could spell drug dealer. To Jammer's mind, insurance adjusters were an even lower form of life than drug dealers or murderers. The trouble was that insurance guys were too boring to write about.

Jammer picked up speed and headed toward the front gate. Directly ahead of him, the cats were bunched in front of Mrs. Moore's door. Oh, oh! Beyond the cats, Jammer saw that the front gate was wide open. A week ago, the lock had been jimmied, and he had put off fixing it because he was so hot on his script. Well, no time now. He picked up speed and sailed, knees flexed in perfect form, over the cats, hitting the sidewalk in front of the gate four seconds later and rolling to a stop. The cats had begun to flee when he headed for them, but he'd cleared them with room to spare.

Jammer rolled back to shut the gate. The cats were returning. He let the board roll him inside the courtyard and stared at the scene unfolding before him. The cats were rearranging themselves on top of the body of a man who lay face up on the terra-cotta tiles. The man wore a dark blue sport jacket, yellow polo shirt, gray slacks, and black shoes. He looked old, but not as old as the Clevelands or Alphonse Fredericks. His arms were folded comfortably across his chest, as though he might be napping or sleeping one off. Jammer could smell booze. But there was a bloody gash on his forehead, his eyes were wide open, and he did not protest as the cats climbed aboard.

Jammer thought maybe he should do something. Stick two fingers on the man's neck like he'd seen on TV? Call 911? As he came closer, the cats moved away and Jammer saw something protruding from the man's chest. A red stain spread from it, covering the designer logo on the left pocket of the yellow polo shirt. Jammer was struck by how silent the courtyard suddenly seemed. Even the cats were quiet. They seemed to be waiting for him to do something. Then, to Jammer's right, the door of number one opened. Mrs. Moore appeared with the gardening cart that she used to haul around her mega sacks of kibble. She fished among the gardening tools and pulled out a trowel.

"Good morning, James." Barely glancing at him or the cats, she was focused on the job at hand, feeding the cats. She had poor eyesight, but her little raisin eyes were bright behind the thick glasses. Jammer noticed her slippers had cross-eyed snake heads with red tongues on them. "Good morning, my little dearies," she said to the cats as she bent over and began shoveling out kibble. The cats surged forward as she set down the bowls and straightened up. That was when she caught sight of the body and screamed long and loud. The cats fled, and Jammer caught her just before she hit the ground.

It was mid-afternoon before Jammer got anything to eat. The police tried to reach his brother, questioning the legalities of a sixteen-year-old high school dropout managing a bungalow court, but his brother was on location in Canada. The good part was getting to watch a real homicide detective in action. Jammer dogged his footsteps, taking notes furiously, and was told more than once: "Back off, kid."

The Clevelands had not yet left and, along with Alphonse Fredericks, were attracted by Mrs. Moore's scream. Alert for clues, Jammer thought Mrs. Cleveland's gasp when she saw the body might be construed as a gasp of recognition. Mr. Cleveland wrapped an arm around her and pulled her quickly away. Alphonse Fredericks wore a shocked expression that Jammer thought was overacting. Monica Lexus and Louis St. Grandam did not appear until the police pounded on their doors. Jammer thought that Monica, as hot as he'd ever seen her in red shorts and a tight Hard Rock Café T-shirt, had put on a fake expression of horror when she viewed the body. What you might expect from an actress. St. Grandam had shown the expression of irritation you might expect from an insurance claims adjuster whose boring job was being interrupted by real life.

After the police had gone and the body had been taken away, Jammer felt let down. The detective had not demanded that everyone come down to the station to make statements, or even told them not to leave town. He hadn't said he would be back with search warrants, nor had he seemed suspicious of their alibis. They all claimed to have been home alone all night. They all claimed to have been watching television and to have gone to bed early. Except for Jammer himself who, although he had been alone, had not gone to bed at all. As a result, he knew that some of the tenants were lying. Everyone claimed to have never seen the dead man before. He didn't know about Mrs. Moore.

Jammer was stoked that he got to see the crime scene techs working. One of them remarked that the dead man might have been attacked with more than one weapon.

"Wow!" Jammer said.

"Oh, yeah," said the tech. He pointed toward the dead man's head. "He was bashed front and back with some kind of blunt instrument. And, this thing sticking out of his chest might be some kind of homemade street weapon. We see them all the time. Yank apart a pair of scissors, and you've got two knives. Hard to trace, cheap, disposable. Just sharpen and stab."

The detective appeared by Jammer's shoulder. "Could be a hate crime," he said. "A simple mugging doesn't require so much battery. Most muggers wouldn't waste the energy. Now, back off, kid."

The medical examiner arrived and knelt by the body, wiggling the dead man's leg. "Broken," the medical examiner mumbled.

It was all over too soon for Jammer. He kept as close as he could to the action and overheard the detective tell the medical examiner they could probably settle for a gang of street punks accosting a drunk, beating and robbing him.

"They caught him in the street, got pissed that he wasn't carrying more money, and beat him too much. We found a couple poker chips, so maybe the guy lost big at a poker game. No ID, no watch or jewelry. Doesn't look the Rolex type. The punks got diddly and didn't like it. What's with the leg?"

The medical examiner shrugged and told the detective he'd have the autopsy report in about a week. Jeez, thought Jammer, a week? He wanted to know now. It could be crucial to his screenplay.

Jammer got the detective alone and hinted that the tenants might know more than they were telling, but the detective had not been interested.

"I'll be in touch," the detective had said with that amused smile on his face.

As far as Jammer could tell, a murder victim found in their own backyard did not have much of a dampening effect on his tenants. But there was a general clamor for him to get the gate lock fixed.

"God forbid we should all be murdered in our beds," moaned Mrs. Cleveland.

Mr. Cleveland complained they'd missed the prime time for celeb sightings on the Strip and now they might as well not bother to go out. The Clevelands had tried to get the police to pose with the dead man. When that failed, they had snapped surreptitiously from behind the banana palms.

Monica Lexus, still looking as hot as Jammer had ever seen her, complained that she was going to be sooo tired at work tonight. Louis St. Grandam had circled the court scowling and shouting into his cell phone until he was allowed to go sit in his car out front and continue his business.

Alphonse Fredericks used the occasion to ham it up, playing some old role. Probably the only role he'd ever had, Jammer thought. Mrs. Moore was prostrate in her bed, and if she had answered any questions, Jammer had not been allowed in to hear them. With all the commotion, her cats had fled back to the hills unfed and hungry.

Jammer ordered a pizza. He was depressed. Seeing how mundane a real murder investigation actually was had killed his enthusiasm for his screenplay. When he told the detective that he was a writer and asked if he could talk to him in the future, maybe ride along on an investigation so he could get the real life flavor of homicide work, the detective had seemed amused. But he handed Jammer his card and said, "Sure, kid, we'll talk."

Jammer sat on his front step and munched pizza, turning the detective's card over in his hand. He read the name, *Detective James McKelvey*. Hey, that was a way cool coincidence. The same first name as his detective hero, as well as his own. Jammer felt a renewed interest.

He scanned the empty courtyard. With some satisfaction he viewed the chalk outline where the body had lain, but he thought it could use a little touching up to actually look like the shape of a body. The crime scene techs had been good, though. They had collected everything in the vicinity of the body in bags, including all the spilled kibble, and loaded it in their vans.

He went back over the day's events, rewriting it in his head, making the mundane more dramatic. He thought there might be some material he could use. He let his mind play the "what if" game. *What if* this real life dead man had been known by someone who lived in the bungalow court. *What if* someone in this court had killed him.

Jammer got out his notebook and tried the murderer's role on each of the court's tenants. There were varying degrees of fit, but he thought it was possible that any of them could have done it. They were all home last night, but they had lied about what they had been doing. *Note: Find out about Mrs. Moore.*

The murder happened on Wednesday night, the Cleveland's night for the mysterious men's meeting, and Jammer had seen at least one man enter their house that night. But he couldn't swear it was the victim. What *had* been going on? Why had he never wondered about these nights before? If Mrs. Cleveland were about forty years younger, you could figure Mr. Cleveland for a pimp, and pimps were notorious for murdering johns. Jammer doubted that was the case here.

Well after midnight he had seen two silhouettes on the blinds of Alphonse Fredericks's window. They seemed to be pacing back and forth as Jammer was himself. Arguing?

Jammer had seen Monica Lexus locked in an embrace in the cone of light outside her door. Had this been the victim? Had he tried something and Monica bashed him? What about the guy's broken leg? What about the knife in the chest?

What about Louis St. Grandam? Last night, when Jammer stepped outside to get some air, St. Grandam had rushed past him and into his bungalow. What time? Jammer didn't know because just then his head had cleared, and he had dashed inside himself with a brainstorm for the screenplay.

Jammer had to admit that he had heard nothing unusual during the night. Plenty of loud music, canned TV laughter, screams and gunshots, the chop-chop of helicopters overhead, sirens, the screech of brakes, the normal background noise of the city. To Jammer it was like the lulling sound of the ocean or the wind whistling in mountain pines. A night person, he was up and around all night and every night. He didn't miss much, but he clearly missed something.

Jammer wrote in his notebook. *Fact: The tenants lied to Detective McKelvey about being home alone, watching TV, and going to bed early.* Did Mrs. Moore lie? Was she home alone like she usually was? Did she have a visitor? Needs investigation.

Fact: The tenants are hiding something. What?

Jammer stretched. The sun had disappeared from the court-yard, and the air was chilly. He carried the empty pizza box to the alley and stuffed it in a trash can. He wondered if he should look through the trash for clues, but the cans were rank and overflowing. He walked back to his bungalow casting a suspicious eye at each of his tenant's bungalows. Lights were on in all of them except Mrs. Moore's. He wondered if he should knock on her door to see if she was all right. Or to see if maybe she had skipped town. After all, she was the original murderer in his screenplay.

Next day, Jammer had four different endings for his screenplay. Somewhere in the wee hours he knew that he was writing with the idea of solving the murder.

In scenario number one, the Clevelands did it. Mr. Cleveland had hit him with a bowling trophy, and Mrs. Cleveland had stabbed him with her mending scissors, breaking them in the process. The victim discovered they had been cheating him in poker and attacked them in a rage. Technically, they could claim self-defense, but they didn't want their game exposed, because they were wanted for the same thing back in Detroit. They had emptied his pockets to make it look like a robbery and dragged him outside the gate. But, he wasn't dead and tried to crawl back to his killers' door, dying just inside the gate. This didn't account for the broken leg, but he'd figure that out later.

In the second scenario, Alphonse Fredericks did it. The silhouettes he'd seen pacing back and forth could have been Fredericks and the victim. He was an angry customer maimed by one of Fredericks's mail order S&M specials. They had fought, and Fredericks had stabbed the man with a spiked jock strap. The man had stumbled outside and fallen just inside the gate, hitting his head and bleeding to death. Maybe the fall was hard enough to account for the broken leg. Fredericks had opened the gate to make it look as though it was an outside job.

In scenario number three, after the victim had brought Monica Lexus home from the Hard Rock Café, she had fed him Scotch and cleaned out his pockets. She planned to send him home in a taxi, hoping he'd think he had lost his wallet. But, she hadn't known how much cocaine he had snorted before they got to her place, where he had many more snorts. She got him out the door and set him stumbling toward the gate, but his heart seized up and he collapsed. She dismissed the taxi and drove the guy's car blocks away, leaving the gate open in her panic when she came back.

Scenario number four was the hardest for Jammer to write. He could easily imagine why any number of people would want to kill a turd like Louis St. Grandam. An insurance claims adjuster who lounged in a BMW all day denying people's claims over his cell phone, for God's sake, was just asking for it. But that was the problem, St. Grandam had screwed up hundreds of people's lives big time. Maybe thousands. But there was only one victim. With St. Grandam it would be more like a scene from *Night of the Living Dead*, with hordes of his victims lurching after him on crutches with bandaged heads and casts on their arms and legs.

Which reminded him that the dead guy had a broken leg.

Jammer jumped off the couch and ran to the window. He yanked up the blind and stared out into the courtyard. The cats were out there waiting for breakfast, sitting on the chalk line where the body had lain. It was just inside the gate in front of Mrs. Moore's door. How many feet was that from the street? Jammer ran outside, scattering the cats.

Starting from the chalk outline of the foot and putting one size thirteen unlaced hi-top in front of the other, Jammer paced off the distance to the street. Twenty paces. Back inside, he stood in the middle of the body outline and looked toward the street. Guy gets hit by a car and is thrown through the air. Twenty feet, no sweat. Takes care of the broken leg and the bash on the head, but not the knife.

The cats crept back, watching Jammer standing still as stone as he worked on the plot. Louis St. Grandam, driving home late after receiving an award for denying 100% of all claims, hits this guy and bounces him into his own courtyard. He checks the BMW for damage and parks across the street to hide the dented fender. He walks past the victim, pausing only to make sure the guy is dead, and goes to bed.

What about the stab wound? Okay, what if the guy was stabbed before he gets hit in the street? Mrs. Cleveland with the scissors, Fredericks with the spike. Then there would be two murderers. Bashed by Cleveland and Monica before he was stabbed and hit by St. Grandam. Yeah, he liked that. Throw in the booze and cocaine anyway. What did they call it when somebody died because you gave them something you didn't know could kill them, but you should have? Criminal negligence, maybe that was it.

Jammer glanced around him. He was surrounded by cats. He was inside the chalk outline, and they were outside it like there was a body shaped moat between them.

Jammer felt satisfied. His scenario fit the facts. Detective McKelvey's theory was that the guy was killed by a gang. Jammer's fictional killers were a gang of sorts. The Clevelands, Fredericks, Monica Lexus, Louis St. Grandam. The bungalow gang. Jammer fished Detective McKelvey's card out of his pocket. He knew Detective McKelvey's theory was probably right, but the detective might advise Jammer on his fictional scenario. He wondered if it was too early to call him. Maybe he would like to be listed as a consultant in the credits when Jammer's film came out.

Jammer looked at Mrs. Moore's door. He thought he heard her stirring behind it. He hadn't figured out a role for her in his story. Originally, she had been the murderer. He liked the new script better. It reminded him of some old movie he'd seen where everybody killed some guy because they all hated him.

Jammer was still standing in the chalk outline, busy casting his film with famous actors, when Mrs. Moore opened her door.

"Good morning, James." She pushed the gardening cart ahead of her and the cats surged forward. "My, aren't you children hungry!" A pregnant female clawed her way up the side of the cart and began ripping at the kibble bag, spilling it.

"Oh, dear." The cats swarmed.

Jammer stepped forward. "Let me help you. It'll go faster if I pour it into the bowls."

"Thank you, dear. The little darlings depend on me so." Mrs. Moore beamed as Jammer pulled the huge bag out of the cart, bringing gardening tools clattering to the tiles. An odd tool came to rest against Jammer's toe. Not quite pruning shears, not quite a knife. Cheap, disposable, hard to trace. He had seen the other half yesterday morning stuck in the dead guy's chest. He looked at Mrs. Moore. The cats were getting impatient; the pregnant female boldly clawing at the bag of kibble Jammer held.

"Go ahead and feed them, dear," Mrs. Moore said. "He was not a nice man." They both glanced down at the chalk outline as if the body was still there. "We certainly found that out last night. But our poor Monica couldn't have known that when she let him give her a ride home. She took him over to the Clevelands for a nice little game of cards. Mr. Fredericks was there too. I don't play myself; I can't concentrate." She fluttered her hands in the air as if to illustrate her card playing disability.

"They told me the man was a poor loser, that he claimed the Clevelands were cheating and attacked them. Mr. Cleveland had to hit him. But what a brute the man was. It didn't faze him and, drunk as he was, he tried to take advantage of Monica in the kitchen. She had to defend herself. But even after she broke the bottle of Scotch over his head, he wanted another drink and blamed her for wasting it. They tried to get him to leave, but he picked up one of Mr. Fredericks's little toys, one of those sharp dog collar things, and threatened him with it. He blamed Mr. Fredericks when he got hurt himself."

Mrs. Moore shook her head at the injustice of it.

"After they pushed him out the door, he obviously wandered into the street because poor Mr. St. Grandam accidentally hit him with his car. You hear about those cell phones causing all kinds of accidents, but I'm sure it was the man's fault." Her black button eyes held Jammer's.

"Still, the man wasn't hurt too badly, because he managed to get to my door. But he wasn't very steady on his feet as you can imagine. He tripped over my kitties and fell down. Naturally, he scared them, and they hissed at him. He swore he would have the cats destroyed after he turned us all in to the police. I had to stop him. I had my pruning shears in my hand. They broke."

Mrs. Moore paused and smiled. "I'm sure you understand; the others did. Such good neighbors; they got him off my porch, emptied his pockets. We couldn't bring ourselves to pull out the shears. I don't remember who thought of leaving the gate open, but it was a blessing that you had forgotten to fix the lock, dear. Later, I'm afraid I had forgotten he was out here. I never like to dwell on bad things."

Jammer thought there wasn't much point in filling bowls. The kibble was pouring out of the bag from numerous tears. He dumped the rest on top of the chalk outline, and the cats dug in. Detective McKelvey's card had fluttered to the ground and lay among the gardening tools. Jammer picked it up and stuck it in his pocket, thinking it was no time to break Personal Rule Number One: *Live and let live.* He gathered up the gardening tools and put them in the bottom of the cart. He stuffed the empty bag on top.

Gayle McGary is a painter and sculptor who exhibits her work under the name Partlow. She designed the covers for Sisters in Crime/Los Angeles's first edition of Desserticide *and their anthology of mystery stories,* Murder by Thirteen. *She teaches art at Los Angeles City College, which happens to be located in Jammer's neighborhood. She has three kids and lives in Altadena with some cats, a crow named Eddie, and her husband Richard Partlow, also a writer.*

COPYCAT

Joan Myers

The thing is, I'm not the least bit creative. I just slog along in the footsteps of others, recognizing individuality when I see it, but wholly unable to do anything but imitate. I copy all my decorative schemes from *Better Homes and Gardens*, and I've learned, after a series of unfortunate mismatches, to change nothing. For the same reason, I follow recipes right down to the gnat's eyebrow. Adding a pinch of this or a dash of that to improve the flavor always results in disaster. My thank-you notes are copied from a book of letters I inherited from my mother. Since it was written in the thirties, the notes are somewhat outdated, so I do make a few changes to fit the circumstances. When I don't forget. My mother-in-law had plenty to say about that the Christmas she sent us that horrible vase that looked like it came from a garage sale (if I know her, it did). I wrote and thanked her for the pillowcases because that was what the form letter said. I wasn't thinking, okay? I had something else on my mind at the time. I can't remember what.

My husband, Hank, used to kid me about it. He was a great

kidder, Hank. He kidded everyone about everything, never allowing even the teensiest foible to go by unnoticed. So when he got his head bashed in, no one was surprised. I don't mean it was expected, of course. Who expects someone he knows to have his head bashed in? What I mean is, it wasn't so unbelievable that someone had been angry enough at Hank to kill him. In fact, Abbey's husband, Chase, said something like that at the wake. I wasn't supposed to hear, of course, but Chase has kind of a loud voice, and it's loud even when he thinks he's lowered it.

The day Hank got himself murdered, I had gone to Costco. We were out of soda, and Hank drank it almost constantly on the weekend. We were low on coffee, too, and cereal. It's a discount store, and they have books there and all kinds of stuff in addition to groceries. I spent quite awhile browsing around, then decided to stop and get a frozen mocha at Starbucks. By the time I got home, I'd been gone two hours.

As usual, I came into the family room through the side door, and I saw Hank through the sliding glass door that opened into the backyard. He was lying face down on the grass next to the withered corpse of a shrub he'd been digging up. The shovel lay nearby, the shrub still in place. I ran out and shook him, but he just flopped around, so I went in and called 911. Then I went back out and put my fingers on his neck the way they do in the movies, but I couldn't feel anything. My stomach was churning, and when I saw his head, mashed all flat in the back, I lost that frozen mocha and my lunch besides.

There was no way he could have been alive, but I turned him over and started CPR anyway. I wasn't thinking too clearly. I didn't do too well with the CPR either, I don't think. I couldn't remember how many times I was supposed to push on his chest before blowing into his mouth, and I kept losing count.

The cops weren't happy at all about my turning him over, nor about the pool of vomit they found next to the body. They acted like I'd contaminated the crime scene deliberately. I watch *NYPD Blue* and *Homicide* religiously, and I love to read mysteries, but I swear I never thought of my backyard as a crime scene. I told the cops I thought he'd fallen and hit his head on the table or something and they looked at me like I was nuts. Okay, the table was on the patio, several feet away. So who thinks clearly with their husband lying dead in the backyard?

Of course, I was the primary suspect. The wife always is. I showed them the case of 7-UP lying on the family room floor where I'd dropped it when I saw him. And the two-pound can of coffee that had been sitting on top of it. The rest of the stuff was in the trunk, and I totally forgot about it until they asked me where I'd been. I should think that would have proved to them that I was out of the house when it happened, but they still gave me those fishy stares, like they were measuring me for stripes, or whatever they wear in prison nowadays.

"I only went to get the soda," I told them. "But I remembered I didn't have any coffee, either. I was running low on laundry detergent, and then I saw that they had fresh corn, and I realized I didn't have anything for a vegetable, and my mother always served all five basic food groups for every meal, which is a good idea, don't you think?" I knew I was babbling, but I couldn't seem to stop. I wasn't really operating on all cylinders.

"Hank loves corn on the cob," I went on while the two detectives from the Orange County Sheriff's Department exchanged looks. "And he always eats two ears. I know he's a little overweight, I probably shouldn't encourage him, but he likes to have chips and salsa when he's watching TV, and we were almost out. That's why it took me so long."

I remembered the rest of the groceries were still in the car, and I jumped up to go get them. My heart felt like a hammer in my chest, and I couldn't seem to sit still.

"Where are you going?"

"The corn. It's still in the trunk."

"Your husband's dead, Mrs. Pauly. You're worried about corn?" It was the tall, good-looking one who said this, his face full of disapproval.

"I guess it doesn't matter, does it?" I said. "He'll never eat it anyway." I know I was supposed to burst into tears then, but the tears didn't come. Later, after the detectives left and Abbey and Kathy came over, I cried up a storm from sheer nervous tension, but while the detectives looked at me with their cynical smiles and their obvious suspicions, I just felt numb.

Then they wanted me to go over the whole thing again, in my own words.

Well, what could I say? Hank had gone out to the back yard to dig up the shrub. I'd already shown them the bush, still in the ground, the shovel lying next to it, a small pile of dirt nearby. He'd barely removed one or two shovels full of dirt when he was interrupted.

The younger detective pounced. "How do you know he was interrupted?" According to his ID, his name was Antonio Perez, and he was getting less good-looking by the minute.

At first I didn't know what to say. Wasn't it obvious?

"Because the bush is still there," I answered. "If he hadn't been interrupted, he would have finished digging it out."

We'd been at this for more than an hour, and I was getting tired of it. Not only the questions, but everything. My yard and my house were full of people, my house had been searched, and in the backyard deputies were pulling shrubs and ferns every which way and digging up the flowerbeds. I assumed they were looking for the murder weapon. Apparently the shovel, another logical suspect besides me, was not a contender. The driveway and the curb in front of my house were full of police vehicles, and a clot of neighbors stood across the street in the Morrow's driveway, looking at the house and whispering among themselves.

"Someone must have come to the door, someone he invited in and then took out to the back, someone he knew," I told the older detective. He was shorter than Perez and had a bulbous nose full of acne scars. His name-tag said "Martin O'Connor." I thought the explanation was obvious, but they looked skeptical.

"We'll check that, of course. We have detectives canvassing the neighbors right now."

Wonderful.

"If anyone did come to the door, someone would have seen him. I noticed when we drove up that there were quite a few people on the street," O'Connor told me.

Well, of course. The ambulance, siren screaming, had arrived fifteen minutes before the detectives. Naturally everyone had piled outdoors to see what was going on. The phone had rung several times already—answered by a sheriff's deputy; I couldn't even answer my own phone, and Abbey and Kathy had been turned away by the policewoman stationed at the end of the driveway. It had been a relief to see them there. Everyone was so mad at us, I wasn't sure anyone would care whether Hank was dead or not.

"I just can't believe he was murdered. Are you sure he didn't hit his head?" I asked. "He might have tripped and fallen, and whoever was here might have panicked and run away." Perez shook his head, the corner of his mouth turned down, as though in contempt.

"Not possible, according to the coroner," O'Connor informed

me. I wondered what else the coroner had said.

"Okay," he said, flipping the pages of his notebook. "You say you didn't do it. So who did?"

"What?"

"Well, someone did it. This was no accident. So who do you know who might have wanted him dead?"

Well, that put me into a quandary. There were the obvious ones, of course. His business partner and the ex-wife who hated his guts. The detectives would find out about them whether I mentioned them or not, so I had no qualms about spilling those particular beans. But I had no idea whether anyone would tell them about Larry Skinner.

Everyone in the neighborhood had been at Andrea's wake when Larry, his eyes nearly swollen shut with weeping, came up to where we stood by ourselves, and told Hank he was going to kill him.

"Get out," he'd screamed. "How dare you come here, you sadistic bastard. You're responsible for this, and you know it." He'd choked then and bent over coughing and gasping. When he was able to resume breathing, he went on in a low menacing voice. "I'm going to kill you," he snarled, his face full of rage and grief. "When you least expect it. You'll never know what hit you. Now get out. And if I see you at the funeral, I swear to God, I'll break every bone in your body."

Larry sounded like a bad movie, but for once in his life, Hank had no smart-ass comeback. White-faced, he turned and walked out the door. I checked Abbey out and was relieved to see she looked merely sorrowful, without that stare of condemnation I saw on the other faces in the room. Experience told me that although they might forgive—after awhile—they'd never forget. They'd be looking for further insult and, Hank being Hank, they'd find it sooner or later. It would be hard enough to be ostracized by the other neighbors, but I didn't think I could bear it if I lost Abbey's friendship.

I've said before that Hank was a great kidder. He'd pulled one of his numbers on Larry, and a little over a month later, Andrea swallowed an entire prescription of Valium. Since then we'd been the pariahs of the neighborhood.

What happened was this. Picture it.

It's Fourth of July, and we're all over at Larry and Andrea's. They didn't want to have the party that year, since it was so soon after Andrea's miscarriage and subsequent breakdown, but we all thought it would be good for her, so we goaded them into taking their turn.

It's getting late. The wine bottles are nearly empty, and three or four cans of beer float in the melting ice in the tub next to the barbecue.

Andrea and Larry are the youngest couple on the block and the only ones without children. The rest of us are empty nesters except for Kathy and Ray, who still have two adolescent girls at home. I have one son, Jerry, by a previous marriage. Hank's only son died of a drug overdose about a year after we were married, which was when he started to turn mean. Hank and Jerry were friends at first, but now I have to go up to L.A. to see Jerry, since he refuses to be in the same room with Hank anymore. But that's another story.

Andrea is desperate to have kids but for some reason can't carry them to term. She's had three miscarriages in the past, all in the early months, and she was eight months along with the latest one when she stopped feeling movement. They told her the baby was dead and removed it by C-section. She came back from the hospital looking like death warmed over, and rejecting all attempts to comfort or divert her. Then one day Larry came home and found her standing on the curb, without a stitch on, showing passers-by her scar. She'd spent six months in the psychiatric ward at UC Irvine Medical Center. At the time of the party and Hank's little joke, she'd been home three weeks.

Hank has been fairly quiet, except for telling Abbey, who was dressed entirely in yellow, that she looked like a fireplug. Nice, huh? Unfortunately, Abbey's constant dieting seems to have no effect on her stocky, nearly waistless figure.

We're talking about movies, about how so many plots are based on marital infidelity, those that don't hinge on impending planetary annihilation, that is. As usual, the mere mention of adultery sets Larry off, and he starts pontificating about morals and family values, deploring the lack thereof. I look over at Hank, and he's got that manic gleam in his eye. I start talking, hoping to divert attention away from him, but that never did work.

Hank starts singing "Little White Lies," which could mean anything or nothing, and Larry's face turns a mottled red.

"What's that supposed to mean?" he shouts, all belligerent.

Andrea's smoking at the other end of the patio. I notice that the pack she opened right after we arrived is nearly empty, and the fact that no one has suggested she's committing slow suicide by asphyxiation is evidence of the general awareness of her fragility. At the tone of her husband's voice she turns and stares.

Hank smiles his Cheshire cat smile. "I saw you," he says and then loses the smile, face serious, eyes alight with malice. "Or maybe it wasn't really you in that blue Camry with the license plate that says 'LAR AND.'"

"What?"

"Last Saturday afternoon? Pulling into the parking lot at TGIF up in Fullerton?"

Last Saturday Abbey and I took Andrea to the movies because Larry told us he had to work and didn't want to leave her alone.

"I suppose that was your secretary snuggled up next to you in the front seat," Hank adds.

As everyone knows, Hank is perfectly capable of making up the whole story, and I, for one, am sure he has. So all Larry has to do is laugh it off and Hank will give up and switch subjects or victims. We all know that by now, and I don't understand why Larry takes him so seriously.

He clenches his fists and takes a step toward Hank. "That's bullshit, and you know it."

"Sure. Sure. You're innocent as a lit-tul lamb." Hank is smirking, full of himself now that he's goaded Larry into taking the bait.

Andrea has a look on her face that—I don't know, exactly—it's like she's solved some perplexing mystery all of a sudden.

Kathy's husband, Ray, grabs a beer, pops it, and holds it out to Larry. Everyone else is riveted, like they can't believe it.

"Don't pay any attention to him, man," Ray says. "You know how he is."

Larry grabs the can, and for a minute I think he's going to throw it in Hank's face.

I check out Andrea, and I don't like the expression on her face one bit. The comprehension that dawned has died, leaving a frightening emptiness. Although the damage has already been done, I stand and tell Hank to shut up, as though he'll pay attention if I'm standing. What I really want to do is put my hands around his throat and squeeze till his eyes bug out.

Again, I cut my eyes toward Andrea. Hank's oblivious, of course, but Larry catches my signal and forces out a laugh. "You're a real card, Hank," he says, as though going along with the joke. Too late, though.

After a minute or two, everyone starts talking again and the incident is over. But Andrea continues to stare at Larry, looking as though someone has punched her very hard in the gut.

Kathy and I go over to her and offer assurances that Hank has been, as he so often puts it, "just kidding," that "it didn't mean anything." After years of hearing him say that to me, I know how meaningless it is, but I don't know what else to say. Andrea isn't listening to us anyway. She looks as shattered as she did when she returned home from the hospital after losing her baby.

"She's not going to have to go back to the loony bin, is she?" Hank asked, not bothering to lower his voice.

"Hank, you asshole," I say.

I doubt Hank gives Andrea a thought. His only motive, I'm sure, is to take Larry down a peg or two. He never thinks about the consequences before he opens his mouth, and this isn't the first time he's put his foot in it, although no one has committed suicide over one of his jokes before.

We've lost friends though. My last best friend, Genelle, the one before Abbey, had stopped speaking to me after Hank came home one evening and started humming "The Too-Fat Polka," which Genelle remembered the words to, unfortunately. Genelle was a little overweight, but not nearly as bad as Hank seemed to think. I don't know why people blame me for his outrages, but they do.

Well, I won't have to worry about that anymore.

Back to the inquisition, where O'Connor and Perez waited for an answer to the question about Hank's enemies. I told them about Hank's business partner and the insurance policy that insured them for two hundred thou each, and the irate ex-wife, with her policy for fifty, and let it go at that. Larry wasn't capable of murder, in spite of his threats, and it didn't seem fair to rat on him. Besides, there was a good chance no one else would mention it to the detectives, and I didn't want to be the stool pigeon in the crowd.

As I wrote down the ex-wife's address, a deputy came in with a large onyx vase Jerry had brought me from Turkey a couple of years ago. The deputy's latest nominee for murder weapon, and not a bad choice either. It had a long narrow neck, perfect for gripping, and it must have weighed ten pounds. The detectives became very excited until they showed it to the coroner, a small Asian man, whom they called Kenny. They stood in the hallway, talking quietly. Kenny looked at the vase and shook his head.

"Too small," I heard him say.

"Too small?" Perez cried, his voice full of outraged incredulity. The vase was large for a vase, but not large enough, apparently, for a murder weapon.

"It has to fit the wound," Kenny said in a voice filled with exasperation. He demonstrated with his hands. "It has to be at least five inches long, three wide with a very shallow curvature." He flipped his hand in a dismissive gesture and turned away.

The vase had been candidate four, or maybe five. I wasn't sure. There had been several likely suspects: my milk glass pitcher, a large rock they'd found in one of the neighbor's yards, a heavy pottery bowl. With each discovery, Kenny's attentions to Hank would be interrupted so he could take part in a low-voiced conversation between him, O'Connor, and whichever deputy had hit what they all hoped would be pay dirt. Occasionally something was bagged, tagged, and put into a box in the front hall, along with all my wastebasket liners and their contents and whatever else the forensics crew deemed interesting. Contents of the trashcans too, I imagine.

The detectives were getting discouraged, I could see. The deputies searched the house and the yard and then, for good measure, the yards of the neighbors on either side and the green belt behind our lot, in case I was stupid enough to whack my husband and throw the weapon over the fence. But despite the overflowing box in the hall, they hadn't found anything really good. As I glanced at the box, I became aware of something lurking at the edges of my memory. It felt ominous, but, try as I might, I couldn't get hold of it.

I wrote out my statement on a yellow pad (just like on *NYPD Blue*) and avoided looking when they bundled Hank into a body bag and carted him away. Shortly after that, Kenny, the forensics team in their white paper suits, and most of the deputies trailed one by one through the front hall and out the door.

The last deputy came in and spoke to O'Connor briefly and quietly, fixed me with accusatory eyes, and left.

To my surprised relief, O'Connor and Perez stood to leave, too. I had thought they would want me to come down to the station for further questioning, but maybe that would come later. In a hurry to see the last of them, I followed them into the front hall, where O'Connor turned and delivered his bombshell.

"You don't happen to have a leg of lamb in your freezer by any chance, do you?"

My heart lurched. "Leg of lamb?"

O'Connor was smiling, but his eyes were watchful. Perez had turned when the older detective spoke, and I felt them both looking at me, rapt as snakes with a cornered mouse.

I managed the wan smile of the recently bereaved, as though I got the joke, but didn't feel like laughing. I didn't fool Perez, though. He pushed past me, headed for the kitchen.

As I turned to follow Perez, the elusive memory returned, and

I realized I had forgotten to put the roast in the oven before I went to Costco. I had turned it on—the oven, I mean—but the phone rang just as I reached for the oven door. It had been Abbey, saying she wanted to make meatballs for dinner but was out of onions and could she come over and borrow one from me.

"I'm just going out," I told her. "I'll bring one over." If she came over, she'd come in through the more convenient side door, as we all did when visiting each other.

"I don't want you to go to that trouble. Hank can give it to me if you're gone when I come."

"Hank is out," I said truthfully.

I had delivered the onion but forgotten the roast. When I came back from Costco, I had been too intent on Hank to enter the kitchen, but the roast undoubtedly still sat on the countertop, thawed by now, most likely, but still bearing bits of Hank, trace evidence, which would be easily discovered by the forensic lab, instead of being destroyed in the oven, like I'd planned.

I thought of bolting through the front door, but how far would I get? And anyway, I could feel O'Connor right behind me. I moved slowly toward the kitchen, expecting Perez's triumphant return with the roast any minute. Icy sweat trickled from armpit to waist and my heart pounded so loudly that I was sure O'Connor could hear it.

At the kitchen door, the rich odor of roasting meat brought relief so acute I nearly smiled. I heard the oven door open, then Perez's anguished curse. He stood at the sink running cold water onto a reddened palm, the oven door still open, the roast just visible. In the oven. Done to a turn, the outside dark and innocuous. I tried to look matter-of-fact, and a little puzzled, as though unaware of their disappointment.

At the front door, the detectives said goodbye and advised me not to leave the county until further notice. I was off the hook. They could suspect me all they wanted, but without the murder weapon, they had no proof. In any case, they didn't have a motive. Or at least not one they'd ever find out about. I'd told them all about Hank's other life insurance policy, the one that named me beneficiary. I had nothing to hide in that regard. Hank was worth more to me alive than dead, as an examination of his business would show. No, my motive had nothing to do with money.

We never eat leg of lamb and all our friends know it, if they remember, so I didn't want to use a leg of lamb, like Barbara Bel Geddes, which would have been much easier, since it could have been swung like a baseball bat. A ham would have been good, but they're rarely frozen, if ever. So I picked a roast, seven pounds and frozen hard as the rock the deputies had confiscated. The roast was unwieldy, but I used two hands, and Hank was bending over at the time with his back toward me. I hit him once, which knocked him down, and a second time for good measure. I couldn't be sure he was dead, because I didn't want to touch him to check his pulse in the unlikely event someone would come into our backyard and find him while I was gone. If the cops got there before I did, and if it was possible to get fingerprints from his neck, I'd have no explanation for mine being there. He looked dead, though. At least he didn't seem to be breathing. It took all the self-control I had to stay out for the two hours I'd allowed myself. I knew it would look suspicious if I didn't call 911 as soon as I came in, and I wanted to blur the time of death a little.

I suppose I was being over-careful, but these were the kinds of things that always tripped up the murderer on *Columbo*. Leaving the roast on the counter would have tripped me up, of course, and I had been sure that's what I'd done. I distinctly remember hanging up the phone, grabbing an onion and my purse and leaving the house in a hurry, in case Abbey decided to come over after all.

Abbey and Kathy showed up with covered dishes before the last cop car had turned the corner. Abbey had a casserole. Kathy brought a salad. They put down their dishes and dispensed hugs and the usual sympathetic phrases. Then Kathy went into the pantry to get a tin of coffee and Abbey told me she'd come over earlier after all.

"I realized after you dropped off the onion that I needed an egg, too. I always forget you need an egg for meatballs until I start to make them. Since you'd already left, I just came in and helped myself. I didn't think you'd mind."

Well, I didn't, of course. We all have keys to each other's houses, and I've borrowed from Abbey, and from Kathy, too, when she wasn't at home.

We stood looking at each other for a moment, while I tried to think of a way to frame the question I wanted to ask.

But Abbey went ahead and gave me the answer. "I put your roast into the oven," she said. "The oven was on, and I assumed you meant to do that before you left."

I nodded. "Thanks," I said.

I didn't know about Kathy, but I knew Abbey had seen that old Hitchcock episode, the one with the murder by leg of lamb. I don't know whether she remembered or not, but I do know that there's no way she could have come into the family room by the side door and not seen Hank lying dead in the back yard.

In any case, I didn't ask her to stay for dinner.

Joan Myers, a retired Medical Technologist, is a former officer of Sisters In Crime/Los Angeles and still an active member. She has completed two mysteries featuring an amateur sleuth who works in a hospital lab. She is married and now lives in Orange County, with neighbors no less supportive than those in "Copycat." This is her first published work of fiction.

MIDNIGHT

Dorothy Rellas

Kenneth Tower sat behind his desk eyeing me with obvious interest. "When you're through in Rome, come back here for a few days. I'd love to show you Paris."

"I don't think Alpha Engineering would okay sightseeing on their time," I said, smiling with as much good nature as I could muster, considering I'd just sat cramped in the middle seat of a plane from Los Angeles for thirteen hours.

A slight tinge of red flashed across his face. Then he sat forward and pressed a button on the intercom: "Send Gus in."

A tall, middle-aged man with dark blond hair and an impassive expression on his ruddy face entered.

"Jenna Albanese—Gus Carlson." Tower picked up two envelopes from his desk and handed them to us. "Tickets for this morning's 10:30 flight to Rome. Gus will fill you in during the flight, Jenna."

I stuffed the envelope inside my tote bag.

"You've been briefed about Russo?" Tower asked.

I nodded. "He's supposed to have stolen Alpha's high-tech

switching system program that the utility industry is interested in."

"There's no doubt he stole it," Tower said. "The data's on a CD that he's turning over to someone named Leslie Conrad, who is selling the program to a European consortium."

Kenneth Tower was over six feet tall, with dark hair, rugged good looks and a tan. Just my type—except I'd never seen him laugh. He looked at me now with the same grave expression on his face I remembered when he'd been my boss as the head of security in Alpha Engineering's Los Angeles headquarters.

"I know all about your friendship with Bill Russo, Jenna."

He whirled a pencil around on top of his desk. "With a personal interest in the case, I'm surprised you were sent to track him down."

That made two of us. My first big assignment at Alpha, and I was stalking my oldest friend. Of course, I knew the problem was merely a fluke. As soon as I found Billy, he'd straighten things out with Alpha before Kenneth Tower overreacted and God knew what would happen.

I tried to match Gus's impassive expression. "What makes you think Bill is in Rome?"

"He's been spotted there. And remember, as soon as you talk to Russo, call Gus. No answering anyone's questions. Gus takes over. You get on the first flight out of Rome. We do the rest."

"What happens to Bill?"

Tower shrugged. "If he's already made delivery, we'll bring charges. If he hasn't, all will be forgiven. Alpha always plays fair with its employees—even the ones who double-cross them."

Outside Tower's office, I explained to Gus that I hadn't had time to pack anything. We agreed to meet in front of Orly after I'd done some shopping.

Gus and I were walking through the airport an hour later. He was as taciturn as he'd been in Kenneth Tower's office. With his slight accent, Scandinavian probably, all he told me was that the unknown Leslie Conrad was paying Bill Russo a couple of million dollars for the program and then would pass it on for his cut—a few million more. By the time we got to the Aer Lingus gate, I was still reeling from the amounts involved.

"Thirty minutes to go," Carlson said. "How about something to eat?"

"Sounds good, but I want to freshen up a bit. I'll meet you at that coffee shop." I pointed to a spot a few feet away.

He nodded, and I pushed through the crowd to the ladies' room and found an empty stall. Five minutes later I was standing in front of the Swissair gate, wearing the outfit I'd just bought. The bulky clothes added to my one-hundred-twenty pounds, my blond hair was tucked neatly under a dark brown wig, and my face was scrubbed—no makeup, not even lipstick. A pair of trendy, over-size dark glasses was the only concession I'd made to a little glamour.

My heart rate was probably beating two times faster than normal when I finally settled into my seat on the plane. I was ignoring an order from a superior. I'd learned a long time ago to be suspicious of Billy and his motives. What if he actually had stolen the program? And what if he was turning it over to Conrad in Rome? I shivered. I'd be out of a job, struggling as a freelance private eye again and playing the piano in some sleazy biker bar to make enough money to live on.

Billy Russo always kept his vacation plans secret, mostly, I suspected, to make everyone think he led an exciting, adventurous life. Actually, his summer vacations were totally predictable—a couple of weeks in Amsterdam, and a drive to The Hague for the North Sea Jazz Festival. I'd gone with him four years ago. In Amsterdam, we'd visited museums and jazz bars and eaten spectacular food—exactly the itinerary he'd suggested when he'd asked me to go with him this year.

I'd turned him down. But I'd known Billy since we were kids. I knew his habits, what he liked to do and where he'd spend his time. Guaranteed he was in Amsterdam, and I'd find him, eventually. The problem would be to convince him to forget the jazz festival and return home like a good boy so he could explain to the head office the misunderstanding over the program.

When I got to Amsterdam, I rented a car, found another department store and bought some decidedly more stylish outfits. By the time I walked into the Deauville Hotel, I was my usual slim, blonde, foxy self, schlepping a new suitcase behind me and hiding my bloodshot eyes and haggard look behind the dark glasses.

Four years ago Billy and I had stayed at the Deauville. It was reasonable, and according to Billy, when it counted, the owner Jonah DeVeere was discreet. No, DeVeere said when I inquired, Bill Russo wasn't staying there this time.

The Deauville was a few blocks off Dam Rak, Amsterdam's main thoroughfare and within walking distance of the Rembrandt Plein, the park where Billy and I had spent almost every evening.

As soon as I'd unpacked, I went to the park, ordered a drink at the park's bar and found enough people who spoke English to get a list of the jazz clubs in Amsterdam. That night, I checked them out. I didn't find Billy. I spent the next two days canvassing the museums with the same luck. The thought that Tower could be right and Billy was in Rome, sent my nervous system into a tailspin.

On Sunday night, I ordered beer at the Rembrandt Plein's bar and glanced out over the crowd. Tapping my foot in time to the music from an accordion trio that played on a small stage, I tried to think of where to look next. At a heavy-set six-two with dark brown hair and wearing steel-rimmed glasses, Billy wasn't hard to spot when he walked into the park. I felt like clicking my heels. Instead, I picked up my beer and ambled over to him.

"What the hell are you doing here?" he said when he saw me, his expression veering from surprise to suspicion.

"You invited me, remember?"

"You turned me down, remember?"

"I changed my mind. I've been looking all over the damned town for you. How about dinner? I'm starving."

We had chicken satay, cole slaw, and a soft, warm roll at a small bakery a few blocks from the park and talked about the jazz festival that was starting in The Hague in a few days.

"Okay," he said, after we'd ordered chocolate eclairs, "what are you really doing here?"

I sighed. "Alpha thinks you stole the data for one of their big projects—the formula for getting into the exec washroom with a special key card, I think it is."

Billy ignored my try at humor.

"I came up with the theory for the system," he said. "I managed a couple of hundred people and spent over a year sweating through it. It's going to revolutionize the way electricity is bought and switched from one part of a country to another. Alpha gets all the credit and millions from the power companies, and it's my program."

"You were working for Alpha at the time, Billy. I think that makes it their program."

"You know how much they gave me for a bonus last Christmas?"

he asked. "A lousy fifty thousand dollars."

I wanted to laugh. It was more than I made for the entire year.

"Come on, Jen, kick in with me," he said. "I'm gonna get rich on this. We'll buy our own private little island in the Pacific."

How many scrapes had I gotten Billy out of during the years we'd grown up together on our own private little beach in Southern California? I thought he'd changed. But his outrageous behavior had merely been lying dormant all this time, just waiting for the right trigger—a few million big ones.

He leaned forward and grasped my arm. "You used to get really wired over the stuff we did, remember? When we borrowed that dude's Rolls so we could go to the senior prom in style? And the first time you played the piano with Eric's combo, and I gave you the necklace?"

"You took the car out of someone's garage, Bill. And when I drove you to the place in Bel Air, you said you were picking up the woman's mail while she was on vacation. How did I know you broke into her house and lifted her jewelry?"

Billy laughed. "Come on, Jenna. What did you think? I suddenly came up with enough money to walk into Van Cleef and Arpels and buy a diamond and sapphire necklace?"

"Billy," I said, tamping down the feeling of excitement that swept through me at the memories, "they know about Conrad."

"I don't even know about Conrad." He popped the last of the eclair into his mouth. "He called me six months ago, muffled voice and all, and talked me into selling him the program. He had it all planned. Gave me a drop-point here in Amsterdam where he promised we wouldn't even see each other. I left the CD at the spot last weekend. After it checks out, he'll call to tell me where I deliver the two key disks that make the program come together."

"Billy—"

"I'm gonna do it, Jen, with or without you."

It was drizzling when we walked outside, and I hunched down into the raincoat I'd bought when I'd landed in Amsterdam. "I've got a car parked at the Deauville. Be glad to drive you to your hotel."

He shook his head. "I'll see you tomorrow so we can make plans."

I spent the night dreaming about running off with Billy to a tropical island, basking on a sandy beach, and dancing in a funky native night club. A knock on my door woke me at ten o'clock the next morning. Only Billy knew where I was staying, so that's who it had to be, right? Wrong.

It was Gus.

He pushed past me. "Good work—you found Russo. Convinced him to give himself up yet?"

I grabbed my raincoat and put it on over my long T-shirt.

"How did you find me?"

He laughed and sat down in an overstuffed chair in front of the window. I perched on the bed.

"Tower was furious when Los Angeles sent you to work on the case. He wanted to handle things himself. The plan was I take you to Rome, send you off on a false trail, and meet Tower here. We find Russo and follow him to Conrad. When you disappeared at Orly, we figured you'd be here. We spotted you Friday night. And now, you've led us to Russo."

"Tower is here?"

"Waiting for my call." Gus rested his elbows on the chair arms and steepled his fingers in front of his face. "Have you worked your persuasive powers on Russo yet—or met the elusive Leslie Conrad?"

"I haven't seen Conrad, and Billy is thinking over his options."

"Perhaps you won't have much influence over him after all. You are very beautiful," he said, bowing his head slightly, "but even an attractive woman is no competition for millions of dollars."

"Billy is worried," I said, deciding I didn't trust Gus very much. "If I can assure him that he'll just get a slap on the wrist, he'll probably give back the program."

Gus nodded. "Of course. But I need to know your plans so I can assure Tower—"

"You're kidding. Tower routes me to Rome, and now I'm supposed to cooperate with him?"

"We are all working for Alpha," he reminded me.

At this moment, at least. "As soon as I figure out how to rescue the program and Billy, I'll let you know."

He jotted down his number at the Hilton. Ten minutes after Gus left, Billy showed up.

"I give Conrad the rest of the program tonight," he said, sitting in the same chair where Gus had sat. "Think I could borrow your car? I promise I'll drive carefully."

"No, I'll drive. No strings," I added when he began to protest. "I'll take you to your rendezvous, then deliver you wherever you want to go. Although, after hearing that Tower's in town—"

"Kenneth Tower's in Amsterdam?" He sat forward.

"His flunky just paid me a visit. There's still a chance to get out of this, Billy." I told him what Tower had promised me in Paris if the disks were turned over.

"Oh, sure, Jenna. And next year, you're gonna be hired to play the piano at the North Sea Jazz Festival."

He was silent for a minute. "Rent another car and let DeVeere get you out of the Deauville without being seen."

"I'll take care of it," I assured him, inexplicably exhilarated by the thought of being a part of one of Billy's wild schemes again.

I walked him to the door. "Just tell me when and where."

At eight o'clock, I met Billy at an Indonesian restaurant a short distance from the Deauville. The place was shadowy and dingy, with a bar in front and an alcove over it where a combo played very cool, very West Coast-sounding jazz.

I told Billy how DeVeere had rented a classy dark green Saab for me and directed me out of the hotel the same way Billy had gone in and out. "No one saw me, and the car is parked across the street," I told him, sipping my sweet, spicy drink.

Over the *risttafel*, Billy explained that a series of electronic transfers had already put two million dollars in an account he'd set up in the Cayman Islands. At eleven that night, he'd meet Conrad and hand over the key disks. Another two million dollars would be transferred. After he'd had his appearance doctored and he'd zipped off to The Hague for the jazz festival, he'd leave Europe with a new identity, ready to settle down in his island paradise.

His plan sounded like a major gamble to me, but I knew that having money transferred with a flick of a computer key and altering appearances with a snap of a scalpel were commonplace.

We finished eating and had lapsed into a nervous silence when the combo segued into "'Round Midnight."

"Remember the last time we heard that song?"

I wasn't likely to forget. Twelve years ago, Billy and I had been celebrating at a club in Santa Monica. I was leaving the next day to play the piano with Eric's combo in New York. The last piece the band played before we'd left was Thelonius Monk's "'Round Midnight." We'd been walking through the parking lot, still humming the tune, when we'd been mugged.

Standing in front of the baggy-pants gangster, we'd been

paralyzed with fear. The humor of the situation had suddenly hit me, and I'd started laughing. The kid's eyes widened; he was probably wondering what he'd do with a crazy woman. Then I'd screamed something to Billy about not being ready to die yet. The diversion shifted the kid's attention. Billy and I dropped down fast, rolled right into the little weasel, and knocked him off balance.

"I doubt we were in much danger," I said. "The thug was just a kid."

"Yeah, a kid with a gun. When you started screaming, I'm surprised he didn't shoot both of us from shock."

"Just part of my plan. Divert them with hysteria. And Billy, there'll be a lot more memories if you forget this lunacy and go home with me."

I covered his hands with mine, but he pulled them away fast and reached into his jacket pocket for an envelope.

"These are the two key disks. Without this data, the program doesn't go very far." He undid about a half-dozen layers of tape, took out what looked like ordinary high-density disks and handed one to me.

"You hang onto this. I'm delivering the other one to Conrad." He put the disk he held into the envelope and carefully resealed it.

"Billy, you're crazy. What's Conrad gonna do when he discovers you're holding out on him?"

"That disk is my insurance, Jenna. And this." He opened his jacket. A holster was strapped to his chest, and a small revolver peeked out of it.

"By the time Conrad gets the package open, I'll be gone. He'll call, screaming for the missing disk, and after I'm sure he's transferred the rest of the money, I'll deliver it." He glanced at his watch. "Better leave in case he gets here early. And no matter how long it takes," he said, "wait for me in the car."

When I got outside, I walked around in the rain for a few minutes until I was positive no one was following me and then went to the Saab. I sat slumped down, perspiring in spite of the temperature that had dropped thirty degrees since the day before, wondering how I'd let myself become Billy's savior again.

A little before eleven, I made up my mind and got out of the car. I was working for Alpha. This was Billy's life and his decision. But his scheme was stupid. I had about five minutes to convince him it was time for him to grow up.

I hurried across the street, ignoring the rain—and the fact that I'd forgotten the car keys in the ignition. I'd almost reached the restaurant's front door when I heard the sound—two cracks, like a car backfiring—or gun shots. A second later, the restaurant's front door opened and a dozen people streamed out.

My heart took a giant galumph. "Damn you, Billy," I muttered, waiting for the exodus to end.

Inside, the restaurant was empty except for a knot of people standing at a doorway in the rear. When I got to them, I peered down a short hall with a bathroom to one side.

"What happened?" I asked a man who seemed to be in charge. "I was just here with my husband—"

"Yes, I remember." He looked at me, perplexed. "Your husband, he meet a man, and they come back here. Another man at the bar follow. Then the shots."

I edged around the people standing in the doorway. The hall and the bathroom were empty.

"I run to here," the man said from behind me, "and see just one person. He staggers to the outside. Then—nothing."

He was wrong. There was something—a pool of blood on the

bathroom floor and an open rear door.

I rushed outside, my breath caught in my throat over the uncertainty of whether Billy was the victim or the perpetrator. There was no one in the alley, so I hurried toward the street. I almost tripped over a man lying in front of a stairway.

Squatting down, I stared at the back of his head, took a deep breath and rolled him over. The arc of light from a dim yellow bulb hanging over a doorway spotlighted the man's face. Gus Carlson. Dead.

"If you're looking for Russo, he drove off a few seconds ago."

Kenneth Tower loomed over me. I couldn't see the expression on his face, but I could feel the tension in his body. I stood up, my heartbeat thudding.

"Your boyfriend's left you holding the proverbial bag," he said. "Which serves you right. First you disobey our orders to go to Rome, then you don't call us when you find Russo." His words were almost a whisper. "Make things right, Jenna—tell me where you're supposed to meet him."

"I didn't know any of this was going to happen. And I told Gus to let me—"

"All right, have it your way. We'll go to your hotel and wait for him to contact you." He took hold of my arm and began walking, steering me along beside him.

"What about Gus? We can't just leave him."

"We'll worry about Gus after we find Russo."

I stumbled along, trying to focus my thoughts. "There's no reason for Billy to call," I said. Tower didn't answer, so I tried again. "Do you know what happened back there?"

"I was sitting at the bar and heard the shots." Tower said.

When I got to the restroom, Gus was stumbling out the back door. I ran past him to catch Russo."

"You tried to set Billy up in order to get Conrad and the program, is that it?"

"That's our job, Jenna. Too bad you didn't cooperate. Billy tried to kill Conrad, and now he's killed Gus instead."

"Billy would never shoot anyone," I said with more conviction than I felt.

Tower pulled me along beside him. "We've got to find him before he tries to sell the program to someone else and pull the same double-cross."

"You're not listening. Billy wasn't trying to double-cross Conrad, and he didn't kill Gus."

"Maybe you don't know him as well as you think." The tone of his voice was harsh. I doubted he was in the mood for a discussion. And how could I argue about Billy's convoluted logic that led him to steal the program in the first place? And to carry a gun?

By the time we'd walked a block, the rain stopped. My brain started to function again—not enough to figure out what to do, but enough to notice the Singel Canal next to us. Ahead I could see the flower barges floating in the canal and the busy Dam Rak intersection.

We passed houseboats anchored at the water's edge and came to one of the large pleasure crafts that cruised Amsterdam's canals. It was brightly lighted and garishly decorated, and the lilting sound of music drifted out.

A ship's bell chimed nine times—a quarter to twelve. The sounds mingled with the raucous conversation of the people queued up, waiting to join the celebration on the boat. I almost stumbled when I noticed Billy sidling up to the group. He jerked his head toward the boat.

I looked at Tower again. His attention was on the boulevard a few feet in front of us. When we finally stopped for the traffic at

Dam Rak, I took a deep breath, lifted my foot, and brought the heel of my shoe down hard on Tower's instep. He yelped and let go of my arm. I raced back along the sidewalk to the pleasure boat, pushed my way up the gangplank and flashed a smile at the young man collecting invitations. He smiled back and waved me aboard.

On deck, I stood gasping for breath. I was doing it again, deliberately disregarding an order. My future at Alpha was over. And maybe my life, too, if Tower was right and Billy had shot Gus. Before I could come up with any answers, Billy grabbed me.

"Damn you, what happened?" I hissed at him.

He nuzzled his face in my neck and whispered, "If you'd stayed in the car, we'd be on our way to The Hague by now. Let's go before Tower figures out where we are."

He led me up a flight of stairs to the top deck and pulled me into the shadows next to the dark stairway.

I'd been coasting along on nerves for the last half-hour, and when I asked Billy the question, I could hardly get the words out. "Did you kill Gus?"

"Hell, Jen, I may have done a lot of dumb things, but I haven't killed anyone yet. And who's Gus?"

"He works for Tower. He went into the restroom while you were talking to Conrad. Tower was at the bar. By the time he got to the back, you were gone, and Gus was lurching out the door. I found his body in the alley."

"It was just me and Conrad, Jen. We went to the men's room, and I handed over the envelope. I'd just left when I heard the shots. I thought Conrad had somehow gotten the envelope open, noticed I'd held out, and was shooting at me."

I shook my head, my panic forgotten while I tried to make sense out of the story. "You think Gus got there and Conrad shot him?"

Billy shrugged. "I didn't wait to see what happened. There was an opening between the buildings, and I wedged through. When I got out front, I ran to the car. You were gone." He stared at me accusingly. "At least you left the keys inside so I could drive up the block and watch for you to come out. When I saw you and Tower, I left the car and followed you."

"So what's Conrad going to do when he finds out you didn't give him both disks?"

"He'll come after you," a voice behind us said.

I jumped, and Billy wheeled around, holding me close to him. Tower stood at the top of the stairway. The lights from the canal put an eerie halo around his face.

"Your friend has done a number on you again, Russo," he said. "She led me to the park on Friday and tonight, right to you."

"You called me to set up the rendezvous," Billy said, "and your friend Gus pretended to be Conrad."

"That's right. You turn the disks over to him, and I step in to nab you. Too bad I didn't get there before you shot Gus." Tower took a step toward us. "Now, give me the other disk, or I might have to shoot both of you."

"I didn't kill Gus," Billy said, staring at Tower, probably mulling over what he should do. Me? I tried to figure out what was wrong with the scenario.

"The other disk, Russo," Tower repeated.

His command brought it together in one sudden moment of inspiration.

"How do you know how many disks are missing?"

I edged closer to Billy, my arm brushing against his jacket. I felt the outline of the gun in the holster inside.

"Billy didn't know Gus," I went on, figuring it out as I talked, "so he assumed he was turning the envelope over to Conrad. As soon as Billy left, you killed Gus and grabbed the disk. You should have been expecting the CD and two key disks—unless you were Conrad and had picked up the CD last week. By the time you opened the package and saw that there was one key disk missing, Billy was gone."

Kenneth Tower took another step forward, the gun pointed directly at us. "The rest room was kind of cramped, so you got away, Russo. But I want that key disk now. Can't collect my four million without it."

Billy pulled me back until I felt the railing behind us. Now that we'd figured it out, Tower had to get rid of his only two witnesses. I could almost hear the shot and feel myself being tossed overboard, where the cold North Sea would engulf me until one of its treacherous eddies sucked my body down to the bottom. The boat was moving, and the bell started tolling again. I shivered while I counted.

One—two—

A death knell. Shouldn't my life start flashing in front of me about now?

Three—four—

Billy hugged me closer. "It's "'Round Midnight," Jenna," he whispered. "Drop and roll, remember?"

Five—six—

I leaned against Billy's chest, the image in my mind: the two of us—Billy portly now, me out of shape, and both of us over thirty—dropping down and rolling into Kenneth Tower fast enough to knock the gun out of his hand. The picture sent me into a hysterical shriek of laughter.

My outburst had the same effect on Tower that it had on the kid twelve years ago—it startled the hell out of him. His hand wobbled, and his inattention gave me just enough time to reach inside Billy's jacket, whip the revolver out of the holster and scream, at the same time firing a half-dozen times. I missed Tower by a mile, but the noise of the shots and my scream unnerved him enough that Billy was able to lunge at him and get him down on the deck.

Eleven—twelve—

It was midnight.

Kenneth Tower was right about Alpha being fair. He ended up in prison on a half-dozen charges, including murder. I got a raise and a promotion. As usual, Billy talked his way out of the caper. He had to resign, but Alpha promised to look at any new programs he came up with. His first one was a fool-proof key card for the executive washroom at Alpha's Los Angeles headquarters. Billy presented me with a gold-plated prototype.

Dorothy Rellas has had a mystery/suspense novel and several short stories published. She has stories scheduled to appear this year in Murderous Intent Mystery Magazine *and* Futures. *At present, a novel featuring an ex-piano-playing P.I. is making the rounds, and she is working on the second book in this series.*

ABOUT THE EDITORS

Susan B. Casmier

Susan B. Casmier has always preferred to write than to talk. She has written two novels, one of which, *The Body Politic*, is a mystery. She continues to work on a third novel.

After teaching writing skills to college students for 35 years, she retired to establish a private practice in educational therapy, working with people with learning difficulties.

She lives in the San Fernando Valley, happily near her daughter and grandson.

Aljean Harmetz

Aljean Harmetz was on the staff of the *New York Times* for 12 years as the paper's Hollywood correspondent and is the recipient of a Poynter Fellowship from Yale for distinguished journalism.

In 1998 her first novel, *Off the Face of the Earth*, was nominated for a Macavity Award. She is the author of four books on the movies, including the classic *The Making of the Wizard of Oz* and *Round Up the Usual Suspects: The Making of Casablanca*.

The mother of three children, she lives in Los Angeles with her husband and Marlowe, her Shetland sheepdog. She spends her spare time running dog agility courses with Marlowe.

Cynthia Lawrence

With the hardcover publication of *Take-Out City*, Cynthia Lawrence made her debut as a mystery novelist. She has also written short stories for *Alfred Hitchcock's Mystery Magazine* and *Ellery Queen's Mystery Magazine*.

Lawrence first appeared in print as a successful writer for children, when she wrote the original Barbie books for Random House. There were six of these best-sellers, including *Barbie Solves a Mystery*.

Her career in West-Coast advertising has led to major copy-writing awards for clients such as Gallo Wines, Max Factor, and Mattel.

She has taught advertising at UCLA Extension and creative writing at Learning Tree University.

SISTERS IN CRIME MEMBERSHIP

Membership in Sisters in Crime is open to anyone who has a special interest in mystery writing and in supporting the goals of the non-profit organization. Its mission is to "combat discrimination against women in the mystery field, educate publishers and the general public as to the inequities in the treatment of female authors, raise the awareness of their contributions to the field, and promote the professional advancement of women who write mysteries."

There are currently 50 local chapters in the U.S., Canada, and Europe.

For information about joining Sisters in Crime, please contact:

Sisters in Crime
Beth Wasson, Executive Director
PO Box 442124
Lawrence KS 66044-8933
+1 785 842 1325
www.sistersincrime.org

Sisters in Crime/
Los Angeles Chapter
PO Box 251646
Los Angeles CA 90025-9263
+1 213 694 2972
www.sistersincrimela.com

NEED MORE MYSTERIES?

If you enjoyed *A Deadly Dozen*, try UglyTown's other books.

UglyTown Mysteries are available at finer booksellers nationwide or use this coupon to order them direct.

____ **By the Balls: A Novel by Dashiell Loveless**
  0-9663473-0-7 . . . . . . $5.95 US

____ **Five Shots and a Funeral**
  0-9663473-1-5 . . . . . . $6.95 US

____ **A Deadly Dozen**
  0-9663473-2-3 . . . . . $13.00 US

UGLYTOWN
attn: Mail Sales
3325 Wilshire Boulevard
Suite 756
Los Angeles CA 90010-1703
FAX: +1 213 483 5620

Please send me the UglyTown Mysteries I have checked above. I am enclosing $ _____ (please include $3.00 US for the first book and $1.00 US for each book thereafter for postage & handling). Send check or money order. No cash or C.O.D.s please. Prices and numbers are subject to change without notice.

Name _____

Address _____

City _____

State_____ ZIP _____

ALLOW AT LEAST 4 WEEKS FOR DELIVERY

Please contact UglyTown regarding discounts on
multiple-copy orders.

Visit uglytown.com